CASSIE & JASPER

Kidnapped
Cattle

by

Bryn Fleming

WESTWINDS
PRESS®

Library of Congress Cataloging-in-Publication Data

Names: Fleming, Bryn, author.
Title: Cassie and Jasper : kidnapped cattle / by Bryn Fleming.
Other titles: Kidnapped cattle
Description: Portland, Oregon : WestWinds Press, [2016] | Series: Range riders
    | Summary: With her family's ranch struggling financially, twelve-year-old
    Cassie and her best friend Jasper head for the mountains to bring the cattle
    home, but an early snow storm, rustlers, and other dangers turn the weekend
    into a fight for survival.
Identifiers: LCCN 2016006835 (print) | LCCN 2016027306 (ebook) | ISBN
    9781941821954 (pbk.) | ISBN 9781943328659 (e-book) | ISBN
    9781943328666 (hardbound)
Subjects: | CYAC: Cattle drives—Fiction. | Cowgirls—Fiction. | Cowboys—
    Fiction. | Ranch life—Fiction. | Friendship—Fiction. | Survival—Fiction.
Classification: LCC PZ7.F59933 Cao 2016 (print) | LCC PZ7.F59933 (ebook) |
    DDC [Fic]—dc23
LC record available at https://lccn.loc.gov/2016006835

Edited by Michelle McCann
Designed by Vicki Knapton

Published by WestWinds Press®
An imprint of

GRAPHIC ARTS
BOOKS®

P.O. Box 56118
Portland, Oregon 97238-6118
503-254-5591

www.graphicartsbooks.com

Acknowledgments

Thanks to the ranchers of Wheeler County for sharing their stories and to my sister-in-law, Kim, for her Spanish expertise.

Chapter 1

Soaked by the freezing rain, I leaned far out from atop the muddy cut bank over the storm-swollen river. My head was bare, my ponytail swinging drenched and matted.

I scanned the water roiling below me for any sign of Jasper. Logs, branches, a drowned jackrabbit twirling round and round in the current. The cold rain blurred my vision. Then I saw it: Jasper's black cowboy hat.

I watched as it whirled twice around an eddy, following the jackrabbit carcass, catching for a few seconds on a half-submerged juniper branch. Then, whoosh! It hit the rapids. White water grabbed the hat and sucked it under, spit it back up a few yards downstream, then swallowed it again.

Gone.

The cattle bellowed behind me, the cows comforting their calves after the swim across the river. My paint horse, Rowdy, stood beside me at the water's edge, blowing dirty river water from his nostrils and shivering. The cold rain pelted down on us.

I held my breath. The cattle had made it across. Rowdy and I had waded and swum and scrambled onto the bank. I'd watched Jasper's horse, Tigger, pull herself ashore downstream of the rapids, but my friend and his dog were gone.

This was all my fault. I brought us up into the mountains, into the storm: now, the worst may have happened. How could I live with myself?

You're probably wondering how two twelve-year-old ranch kids had gotten themselves into such a predicament. Right?

Here's how it started:

It was early October; the pastures brown and dry and streams barely trickling in their gravel beds. The low autumn sun warmed up the days but nights had a wintry bite.

My best friend, Jasper, from the next ranch over, and I were on our horses, vaccinating calves in the corral by the house.

Jasper's big old blind dog, Willie, lay in the shade near the corral, dozing. I could hear him snore and saw all four of his paws twitch in rabbit-chasing dreams.

The calves we were tending were bummers who'd lost their mothers or been rejected by them. Having lost my own ma, I was a sucker for an orphan, so Jasper and I had bottle-raised them. We kept them down here at the ranch when the rest of the herd was driven up to the mountain pastures last spring.

Jasper and I were giving the bummers their second round of shots. They were like our own little herd, and we were responsible for them. I liked the feeling.

The other calves on the ranch all got branded, vaccinated, and ear-tagged at once. A whole crew came in to help. It was like a party (but not for the cows and their babies, of course.) Ranchers and cowboys moved from ranch to ranch to help get everyone's cattle done each spring.

Sometimes, I pretended the ranch was mine, not my pa's, and the miles of fence were mine to mend, the acres of hay mine to water and cut and bale, the cattle mine to raise and care for and sell.

I was on my horse, Rowdy, although I could have done my part on foot. I loved working cows on horseback. Couldn't get enough. I guess it's in my blood from my pa and my ma before she passed away and their folks before them.

I may be the last in my family of Central Oregon ranchers. In fact, this very ranch was homesteaded by my great-great grandpa when he came over from Arkansas on the Oregon Trail. But that's another story.

My dream has always been to stay on this land working cows forever. Well, for the rest of my life, anyway.

"Get behind him, Jasper," I pointed with my chin at the last calf, my hands being full of lariat and reins.

"¡Claro!" Jasper said. "¡Estoy intentando, Cassie!" Jasper was half Mexican, on his ma's side, a small, wiry, quiet kid, and he lapsed into Spanish sometimes, especially when he got excited.

Jasper wheeled his horse, Tigger, to the left and cut off the calf's escape. Tigger and the black calf had a stare down for a few seconds. Jasper sat low and straight, sunk into the saddle like he'd been working cattle forever. I think he felt best there because his limp didn't show.

Tig stepped forward; the calf stepped back. I urged Rowdy in behind the calf, leaving it nowhere to go. I was a pretty good horsewoman myself, a head taller than Jasper, but not as good with a rope.

Slow and easy, Jasper shook a loop on his rope, dangling it against his leg on the side away from the wary calf. I kept my own rope in my hand, ready if Jasper missed his throw. But he never missed. The calf bawled once as the loop hung in the air then settled over its neck.

"Good job, Jas."

Jasper backed Tig up, tightening the rope between the saddle horn and the calf. The calf ducked his head, struggling against the rope, reared up on his hind legs, then lowered his head and kicked up his small back hooves.

"He's a wild one," I said, admiring the animal's spunk. "He'll be daddy to a lot of good calves when he's grown up."

Between the two of us and the two horses, we finally got the calf to stand with all four feet on the ground. I swung down and hooked my arm around the calf's neck, talking in my most soothing and convincing voice, "It's for your own good."

I stuck the needle in his haunch and pushed the plunger down with my palm.

"Got him," I said.

Jasper snaked the loop loose from where he still sat on Tig. "Maybe you and I could buy this calf and start a herd of our own," he said. "Something to think about."

I slapped the calf lightly on the rump and sent him running back to the others where they were milling around in the corner of the corral.

I unhooked Rowdy's cinch and hauled his saddle off,

propping it against the barn wall. I led him into his corral and took off his bridle. Jasper swung down off Tigger and tied her to the fence rail in the afternoon shade of the barn.

"Our own herd." I considered it out loud. Sounded good. "Start with a couple cows and a bull. Pretty soon they'd have babies. Then we'd have yearlings. Keep the heifers to have more calves, sell the bull calves at auction."

Right now, Jasper and I were just helping out on our families' ranches. Just kids playing cowboy, really. But our own herd, that would be different. A lot of responsibility.

If the cattle fattened and had good calves, we'd make a slim living; if the winters were harsh, the hay got rained on, the calves got scours or worse, we'd lose everything and have to start over. Cattle ranching was a precarious business.

I lifted the handle on the hydrant in the barn-yard and let the cool water rush over my dusty hands. I splashed my face and rubbed the back of my neck, then stood back to let Jasper do the same. He stuck his whole head under the faucet, then turned it off and shook his soaked black hair like a dog coming in from the rain.

"I better get home," he said. "Dad's cooking chili tonight. And corn bread."

"Your favorite."

"Yep." He untied Tig and tucked his left foot in the stirrup and swung his leg over. "See ya on the bus tomorrow. Ven, Willie." The big black dog stood and shook the dust from his coat. He followed Jasper's voice and fell in behind the horse.

"Oh yeah. Monday. Thanks a lot for reminding me." Sitting in school was not my favorite way to spend the day, but you probably already figured that out. Especially this time of year, when the days were getting shorter and there never seemed to be enough time to ride and play after homework and chores. "Wish it was still summer."

Pa stuck his head out the back door as I waved goodbye to Jasper.

Jasper rode up the hill that separated his family's ranch from ours. Willie trotted along behind, following the sound of Tig's hooves scrunching on the dirt track. I watched Jasper smile back at his dog. He sure loved that old guy.

"Cassie," Pa said. His voice warbled odd across the yard, like he had a catch in it. Like when he'd come back from the hospital without my ma two years ago. Like the first time my world fell apart. Seemed like I was only now starting to get it sewn back together.

My heart took an extra thump in my chest, remembering that day. "Yeah, Pa?"

"Would you come in here, please?"

He leaned on one crutch. He'd broken his leg when he fell off his horse a couple weeks ago, the night Mr. Daly's buffalo got into our alfalfa and he and my big sister, Fran, and I had to get them out. But that's another story, too. I've got a lot of 'em for being only a kid.

Anyway, the broken leg seemed to weigh on Pa, making him slow and sad as well as hurt.

"Coming. Just gotta put my saddle away." I'd no more walk away and leave my saddle on the ground than I'd walk out of the house without my clothes on. No good cowboy would.

I carried my saddle by its horn into the barn and put it on its rack, the one with the plaque that said CASSIE in curlicue letters, the one Ma had nailed there when she made the rack for my first saddle. I ran my fingers over the letters and straightened the saddle so the stirrups hung straight. *I sure did miss Ma.*

I headed in to see what was gnawing on Pa now. I had an uneasy feeling in my gut. Usually my gut was right.

Chapter 2

Pa and my sister, Fran, stood in the kitchen when I banged through the back door. Fran stirred a big glass pitcher with a wooden spoon. Pa leaned against the round oak kitchen table where we three ate our meals.

"Cassie, Fran, sit down. I need to tell you girls something important."

My uneasy feeling leaped and clawed in my stomach, a creature waking after hibernation.

Pa pulled a chair out and sank into it. He leaned his crutch against the table edge and stretched his cast-stiffened leg out to one side. He looked at the wounded leg like it belonged to someone else, like it surprised him to see it attached to his hip. His hands crabbed together on the wooden tabletop.

Fran carried the lemonade pitcher to the table. She poured the glasses full and set one in front of Pa and one in front of two other chairs. Ma's place at the far side, across from Pa, sat emptier than ever.

Fran and I sat down. I scuffled my boots under the table and traced a "C" on the dewy surface of my glass.

A triangular silence stretched taut between us, one of those lumps of time that inflates tight as a balloon, but really only lasts a few seconds.

Pa sighed and lifted his head to look us in the eye, my big sister first, and then me. "We're on the edge of losing the ranch," he finally said; a coyote howl of an announcement, defeated and sorrowful.

"The place was all paid for a long time ago, but, well, I've had to borrow against it during bad years. Now there's a mortgage needs to be paid every month."

Money, I thought, in the grown-up world, it was always money.

He went on, "Winter's coming early. Snow level's dropping." He nodded toward the window where we could see the white snow line straight as a ruler across the foothills and the peaks beyond. "The cattle need to be brought down from the mountains right away, before the storms hit." He paused so we'd feel the weight and coldness of the problem.

"I'm in no shape to ride." He knocked his glass gently against the top of his cast, halfway up his thigh, indicating the source of our troubles.

Fran spoke up. "Can't we hire somebody?"

Pa shook his head and smiled a slow, thin-lipped smile. "Truth is, girls, there's no money. With all the rain at cutting time, the hay crop didn't bring much."

Money, again.

His face was slack and dark. "I'll need to sell the herd where they are, take a loss, let the new owners bring them down from the mountains. It's the only way."

I stared at him. "Sell the herd?" The cows and calves had been fattening up on the mountain pastures all summer. Pa and I and the ranch hands usually brought them down to the lower fields for the winter. We sold the young steers to keep us going over the winter and auctioned some of the heifers in the spring.

"What would we live on after that?" Fran asked.

"That's the thing," Pa said. "No cattle, no money, no mortgage payments, no ranch." He tried to lighten his voice then, like he was giving Fran and me some good news, instead of squeezing the life out of us, well, out of me anyway.

"I've been offered a construction job in Bend. We'd move there and I'd start work when my leg healed up."

Fran's face brightened. "Really? Live in the city?"

I knew my sister. I could see it spinning through her mind like a carnival ride; the bigger school, more boys, the movies and malls. She was a traitor to the ranch. I hated her right then.

Me? I felt my face go red and my hands begin to shake. I stood so suddenly, my chair clattered to the floorboards. I didn't care.

"No! Pa, no! We can't leave the ranch!" My throat tightened like I was being strangled. "What about Rowdy and Pet? What about my friends?"

"The horses would have to be sold." Pa didn't meet my stare. "You'd make new friends." He swallowed hard, his Adam's apple rising slowly, and turned even further away.

Fran just sat there, a smug smile cutting her face in two. I wanted to slap her.

I closed my eyes tight, wanting the whole scene to disappear. Fiery tears gathered behind my eyelids. I opened my eyes, let the tears slip down my cheeks, a punishment for Pa, and stomped out.

I grabbed the bridle from the barn and caught Rowdy. He nickered and nuzzled my shirt pocket, looking for a peppermint or a carrot.

"Oh, Rowdy," I pressed my face to his face and felt

his eyelashes whisper across my wet cheek. "How could I ever leave you?"

I couldn't even think about someone else owning my horse; brushing him, riding him, or worse yet, neglecting him. I thought of poor thin Glory, the horse Jasper and I had rescued, saw her sad eyes, ragged coat, and overgrown hooves. No, I couldn't let that happen to Rowdy. I wouldn't.

My hands shook as I buckled his cheek strap and pulled the saddle cinch tight. I lodged my foot in the stirrup and swung up.

My thoughts raced ahead of us as Rowdy and I took down the hill behind our house in long reaching strides. My horse felt my anger, my sadness; I know he did. He knew me deeper than anyone, even Jasper.

When we reached the ridge crest, I pulled Rowdy to a halt. He blew hard and danced in the bunchgrass. I patted his neck under his black mane and kept the reins tight.

I skimmed my eyes over the land below me; the John Day River Valley, Sutton Mountain flat-topped and stern, the distant, darkening humps of the Ochoco Range to the west, the Strawberry Mountains layered green on darker green to the east. The mountains watched over me all my life.

This was my home; the patchwork hay fields, the

river cutting through cliffs. I was part of the land. It made me "Cassie": rider, ranch kid, cowgirl.

I looked around at our neighbors. Jasper's family's ranch hunkered in its bowl just down the winding gravel road from ours. Carter's cattle ranged their pasture where Sutton Mountain leveled out into the valley. The John Day River, flat and calm and green, wound out of the mountains, twisted through the valley, and dwindled away out of sight.

How could I leave this place for city streets and traffic, lights and noise and people everywhere? I'd sooner sleep in a cave in the mountainside with the bats squeaking in and out and the rattlesnakes wanting into my warm bedroll. I'd sit in the mouth of my cave and look down on this valley and no one could ever make me leave.

But I was just a kid. Parents made the decisions. Until I was eighteen, I might as well be in jail for all the choice I had in my fate. I felt angry tears ready to overtake me again, my stomach roiling like I'd eaten something bad.

I swung down off Rowdy and sat cross-legged in the dust on the ridgetop, wiping my runny nose with my sleeve.

There had to be a way to stay. Had to. Had to.

I ran through it in my mind, turning it over like a

piece of river rock, looking for a speck of gold in the gray granite.

Pa's words came back to me: "no money, no ranch." The whole conversation repeated itself painfully in my head, over and over. I thought hard, tried to turn my useless anger into a solution.

If we absolutely had to sell, maybe whoever bought our ranch would let me stay on as a hired hand. After all, I knew every draw and canyon a cow could hide in. I could rope and ride and cook and clean. I'd do anything.

Or maybe I could live at Jasper's. At least I'd still be out here, not in the city. I could keep Rowdy. I could still work cattle. And Jasper's folks were nice.

But, being next door, I'd have to see whatever strangers bought our place coming and going every day, see their horses in our corrals, some other kid getting on the bus at the end of our driveway, knowing her saddle sat on the rack Ma made just for me. Nope; I didn't reckon I could stand it.

"This stinks!" I shook my head and said, "Come on, Rowdy." I stood and swatted the dust from the seat of my jeans and wiped my sleeve across my face again. I wrestled my sadness into determination.

I had to figure it out, but I was drained dry of ideas, like a stock pond at the end of summer: just a little pool of

damp at the bottom, everybody, ranchers and cattle, looking skyward, praying for rain.

I scratched Rowdy under his forelock and whispered, "Let's go see Jasper. Maybe he can think of
something."

Chapter 3

As I rode down the hill, the scene in Jasper's barn-yard was so calm and peaceful, I almost hated to stir it up with my problem. Seemed like I had no choice, though, and what are best friends for? I'd helped Jasper get his dog, Willie, after all. Now I was the one who needed help.

Jasper was brushing Tigger's dun coat with a rubber currycomb, making big circles to loosen the hair and dirt. Tigger munched her hay. Jasper was singing something sweet to his mare as her tail swept the dirt.

Willie drowsed in the shade of the tall poplar tree by the barn. He raised his head and wagged his tail slowly, flop, flop in the dust when he heard Rowdy's step.

Jasper stopped brushing, probably surprised to see me again so soon. "You missed the chili and corn bread."

He rubbed his stomach over his plaid button-down shirt. "Too bad. Sure was good." He knocked the currycomb against his boot, raising a cloud of horse hair and dust. Then he noticed my face. "¿Estás bien, Cassie?"

I was sure my frustration reeked, like stink off a dog that's rolled on a carcass.

I studied my boot tops awhile more, mulling over how to say it. "Worst thing ever," I finally spit out.

"Worst ever?" Jasper shook his head like he doubted me. He led Tigger into the corral and slipped off her halter. "Come in the barn while I soap my saddle."

I plopped down on a straw bale in the barn aisle and watched Jas dip a fat sponge into a pail of water and run it over a tan bar of saddle soap. It smelled like pine tar and summer.

"Well?" he asked, rubbing the sponge over the smooth leather seat of his saddle. "What's got you so wound up?"

"Like I said; worst thing ever."

He stopped rubbing and tilted his head, his eyebrows raised.

I took a deep breath and dived in. "Pa says there's no way to get our cattle down from the mountains before winter, what with him being laid up, and we're out of money and we have to sell the cattle where they are and give up the ranch and move to the city so he can work."

There; I'd said it out loud. The awful reality of it hung in the air, jumbled with the dust and the smell of soap and leather and hay and the delicious warmth of animals well cared for.

Jasper's mouth hung open. "¡No es posible!"

"Yep." I stood up, already feeling closed in, caught in a trap. I paced in and out of the sunlight falling like bars across the barn floor.

"You and me, we have to think of something, some way to raise money to hire help to bring down the cows, or pay the mortgage, at least until we can get the herd down, or . . . or . . . I don't know, something." I kicked the straw bale with the toe of my boot and raised more dust, like more questions floating through the air.

Jasper picked up the sponge, dipped it in the bucket again, and rubbed it on the soap. He picked up a stirrup leather and ran the damp sponge over it slowly, up and down, up and down, both sides of the strap, not saying anything.

"Well?" I nearly shouted. "What are we going to do?" I wanted him to get as mad as I was, to rage and stomp around and agree about how unfair it was. But I knew my friend. That wasn't his way.

Finally, he seemed satisfied that the strap was clean

and soft and supple. He dropped the sponge back in the bucket and leaned his elbow on the saddle on its rack.

He said, "Why don't we just go get the cows, you and me?"

I laughed in spite of my anger and frustration. "What? You and me ride off on our own into the mountains and bring back the whole herd of cattle?"

Jasper nodded.

"You and me and Rowdy and Tigger up in the mountains with the bears and cougars and winter coming on?" I paced back and forth in the barred sunlight. Jasper kept nodding.

"You've been up there, Jasper. You know how rough that country is, all cliffs and gullies and trees so thick you can't see through 'em. Think how many things can go bad and no one around to help if one of us falls or gets snake-bit or we get snowed in or lost . . . a million things could go wrong!"

"Yep," he said. "You got another idea or you want to go home and pack for your move to town?"

"Just you and me bringing down the herd, no grown-ups? I thought you'd come up with a real idea."

I kicked the straw bale harder this time and the twine popped loose and the bale burst and the straw tumbled across the barn floor.

"We're twelve," I reminded him. "Our parents would never in a million years let us go."

"We don't tell them, we don't tell anyone. We'll say we're going on a field trip for school or something. Maybe I can tell my folks I'm staying at your place and you tell your pa you're with me. We could do it over a weekend, be home by Sunday night."

"Right," I shook my head. "What if our folks come looking? It'd never work."

"Hey," Jasper stepped in front of me, stopping my pacing. "You're the one who fought off Carl when we stole the horse, and you're the one who helped me and Willie rescue Ginny from the wildfire. So you don't tell me we can't do it."

He picked up his bridle and sponged Tigger's grassy spit off the bit, then he went on: "Even if our folks figured out we weren't where we said we'd be, they couldn't catch us. Like you said, that's big, rough country up there, miles and miles of it. And we'd have a head start."

Something loosened in my mind, hope muscling aside despair. "Might work," I conceded. "And what could they say when we brought them home?"

Jasper grinned. "We'd come riding in with the whole herd trotting along ahead of us. You could keep the ranch. We'd be heroes!" His eyes flashed bright.

"How many head are we talking about? A hundred, hundred and fifty?"

I considered for a minute, remembering back to last spring when we'd sorted out which cows would go. "Only about forty cow-calf pairs, I think."

"We can do it, Cass." He said it so simply, as if it were already done. "Look." He held up his lucky horseshoe charm on its chain around his neck. "We can do it," he repeated.

I stared out the barn window at the fields stretching away, the mountains starting to color pink with sunset, like I'd find the answer there.

And I did.

"Guess we've got nothing to lose if we try," I finally said, "and everything to lose if we don't."

I stuck out my hand and Jasper took it and we shook on it. We had a plan.

Chapter 4

Cassie, are you with us?" Mrs. Norton's voice roused me out of my daydreams. I sighed, hating to let go. Seemed like there was so much to think about.

I'd been packing my saddlebags in my head, thinking of all the things Jasper and I would need when we set off early next Saturday morning: food, of course, and water for us; the horses could drink from the streams and ponds, but I wasn't going to take a chance on getting beaver fever, bedrolls. . . .

"Cassie, would you please tell us the significance of blah blah blah. . . ."

I couldn't, of course.

"No, not really," I admitted. "Um, could you repeat the question?" Tittering laughter around me and a bigger cough-laugh from the back of the room.

"Please move to the front row, Cassie. We'll see if you can hear me better from there."

I gathered up my books, slow trudged up to the front, and plunked myself down at an empty desk. Mrs. Norton started up again: blah, blah, blah and I drifted back to my saddlebag packing: wire cutters, hoof pick, leather gloves. . . .

I'd been doing a little better in school since Jasper and I had stolen the horse. The importance of getting an education sunk in a layer. I'd seen what dropping out of school had done to Carl McCarthy, the horse's owner, how he'd turned into a criminal. After that, I studied harder, read more, paid attention in class . . . sometimes.

But nobody could expect a person to think about algebra and history when she's getting ready to ride into the mountains and bring back a herd of cattle almost single-handed.

Of course, nobody knew about the plan but me and Jasper, so I could hardly use it as an excuse. Maybe when we came back as the heroes who saved the ranch I'd be excused for doing so poorly in school this week.

Maybe. I didn't really care.

Jasper and I worked on the plan every day. After school, we went over the lists we made, the route we'd take, what we'd do if we encountered x, y, or z unexpected thing. (X = bad weather, y = predators fiercer than us, z = we get hit by lightning.)

That week before the trip, we gathered up the camping gear and extra horse tack and stashed it in an empty stall in the back corner of our barn where no one would see it.

In my room, I stuffed clothes into my backpack, watching over my shoulder for Fran or my pa the whole time. Jeans, T-shirt, flannel shirt, boot socks, blanket coat, sweater . . . hard to say what we'd need up there; fall in the mountains could be warm as summer, could be nice and cool, or could slam us with rain, sleet, or even snow. Nights would be freezing for sure.

Just looking at the snow inching down the mountains every day made me itch to get going. Our cows were up there somewhere. Winter was coming. Pa was ready to give up and sell out. We didn't have much time.

Thursday evening after chores, Jasper and I checked off the list we'd agreed on as we sorted through the provisions in the back stall of my barn. Swallows swooped in and out of the diamond window of the hayloft. Willie whined and scratched at a pack-rat hole under a hay bale. Everything was peaceful and calm. Everything but my insides, and probably Jasper's.

I tried not to show how nervous I was, so I grinned at him as we checked off the last items: flashlights and extra batteries. "We're really doing it!"

"Yep," Jasper nodded. "Day after tomorrow, we'll be gone. You excited?"

"'Course I am. It'll be fun, a piece of cake." I said it, but didn't entirely mean it. I had more than a few worries. Would just we two kids really be able to keep track of the herd? What if they got spooked and scattered? What if one of the horses tripped and broke a leg? Still, I kept my fears to myself—a plan was a plan.

I tried to sound confident. "I remember exactly where we left the cows last spring. There's so much grazing in those meadows, I doubt they've have wandered far. The calves can't cover a whole long distance, anyway."

I went on, remembering the spring cattle drive. "We'll ride on the highway for a mile or so, just to Gable Creek, then about five miles to where the road cuts off to Black Snake Mine." I untied the baling twine around my sleeping bag and rerolled it tighter.

Jasper picked up the trail I was following in my head: "Then past the old gold mine. Do you think we'd have time to dig around there a little? Maybe we'd find some nuggets they missed. . . ." Gold flecks sparkled in Jasper's eyes when he talked about it.

"Maybe one of your ancestors was a miner, Jas. You sure do get excited about gold."

"Remember the field trip to the Blue Bucket Mine? Remember the gold I found?"

"That little flake? I remember how you got in trouble for ditching the group and scratching around in the pile of tailings by the creek. Boy was Mrs. B. mad. She was about ready to get up a search party you'd been gone so long."

Jasper smiled. "Yeah, maybe I'm a miner at heart. But if we stop at the Black Snake on the way to find the cows, I might find a big nugget! Then we could buy our own ranch and cows and. . . ."

At first, I shook my head. His eyes lowered in disappointment. I felt bad; after all, he was helping me. I added, "Maybe just a short break. If we spend all Saturday poking around that old mine, we'll never find the herd before dark. Besides, if there was any gold left, someone would have found it by now."

"Entonces. . . ." Jasper nodded slowly in agreement, but rubbed his hands together like a greedy villain in a movie.

We both laughed.

I found the cook kit in the pile; one pot and a wooden spoon, still crusty from our last camping trip. I scraped it with my thumbnail and smelled it; cheese?

"We're eating mostly cold food, jerky and pemmican, right?"

"You mean that dried fruitcake stuff? Sure," he said, "it's what the mountain men ate, right? Didn't hurt them not to have eggs and flapjacks every morning."

A voice at the barn door made us both jump. "What are you two doing back there?" Fran stood leaning in the doorway. How long had she been there? What had she heard?

I scurried out of the stall like a pack rat caught in the lantern light. I hauled Jasper behind me by his sleeve.

"Nothing, just talking where nobody can spy on us." I squinted hard at her. "What do you want?" I held my breath while she craned her skinny neck to peer over my shoulder to the back of the barn.

"Pa said to see if you did your homework and if you didn't you need to come in right now and do it."

"Tell him I'll be in in a minute," I said.

"Whatever." Fran had delivered her message and turned on her heel and headed back to the house. I guess us kids bored her enough that she couldn't be bothered to snoop any closer.

Jasper exhaled when the back door slammed behind her. "That was close."

"Yep." Too close. I didn't like it. "I better get inside. See you on the bus tomorrow."

"Adios." Jasper whistled, "Come on, Willie." The big

black dog whined and gave a couple more scratches at the pack-rat hole. Jasper tugged gently at the old blind dog's collar. "Nothing wrong with your sniffer, is there?" he said. "Come on home now. That old rat'll be there next time you come, I promise."

"Hey, Cass?" Jasper untied Tigger from the corral fence. "I don't suppose Willie can come, can he?"

I thought about it. Willie was an amazing dog, but he was precious to both of us.

"I don't think so. Too dangerous. A blind dog up in that rugged country? He'll be safer staying at home with your folks."

"Right." Jasper looked at his dog, the one he'd waited so long for and worked so hard to get. I knew it pained him to leave Willie behind. But again he agreed, "Right, too dangerous."

I watched him swing into the saddle and start up the hill with Willie trailing at Tigger's heels. Just two more days and we'd be riding the other way, up into the mountains. We'd find the herd and come riding home as heroes.

I held that vision in my mind: come heck or high water, snow or sleet or bandits or whatever, we'd bring back the herd and save the ranch.

Chapter 5

As we rode out Saturday morning, I swung my feet clear of the stirrups and tipped my hat down to shade my eyes from the sun just rising over the peaks. It was 6:00 A.M. Funny how hard it was to get up for school and how easy it was to jump out of bed to start on an adventure.

We'd finally decided on the "camping at the river" excuse, because it gave us a reason to disappear for the whole weekend and to take the horses with us.

We'd tricked our folks with that excuse once before, when we rescued the horse Glory in the middle of the night. For a while after that "incident," as Pa calls it, it took some convincing to get permission to stay out overnight again. But twice since that night, we'd camped at the river and come home without stealing a horse. So, I guess you could say that our folks hadn't learned their lesson yet, and they let us go.

Pa had only glanced up from his paper when I'd asked him. "A little cold at night for sleeping out, isn't it?" he'd said.

"We like it." I didn't look him in the eye, but fiddled with the fishing fly I'd been tying at the kitchen table. "No mosquitoes, lots of stars."

I figured we had a good chance at success when we rode toward White Butte and the Ochoco Mountains in the thin dawn light. The deck was stacked in our favor, as they say in card playing. I hoped I held a handful of aces.

I knew exactly where we'd left the cattle last spring and I pretty much knew how to get there. Jasper and I were both better riders than most grown-ups. We had two good, strong, sure-footed horses. And Jasper was the best roper I knew. He'd even saved my life with that loop of rope once. (Yep, another story.)

Most of all, we were determined to bring home the cattle and save the ranch. It couldn't be otherwise, or my life was ruined. That's what you call a strong motivation.

We rode down Burnt Ranch Road and hit the highway.

"You get Willie all settled in?" I asked.

"Yep," Jasper nodded glumly, eyes down. "Pobrecito,

he really wanted to come, whined at the gate as I rode off."

"You did the right thing, you know; I love Willie too, but looking after him would just be one more worry."

Jasper sighed and patted Tigger's neck. He loved his animals fiercely. We both did.

"Willie and I have hardly been apart since I brought him home from the shelter," Jasper said, "except for when I'm at school. And he's always waiting for me when I get home, big ol' tongue hanging out, tail wagging."

We rode on a ways in silence, the morning unfolding around us. First light shone on the peaks, yellow and soft. Robins picked dusty juniper berries and flew off with them in their beaks. Meadowlarks called to each other from fence posts and treetops.

"Imagine the look on your pa's face, and Fran's, too, when we herd the cows up the driveway," Jasper said.

"Yeah," I agreed. "Pa can't possibly be mad when he sees that we've saved the ranch." I just hoped we didn't get caught before we'd barely gotten started.

I looked behind us a few times, back the way we'd come, back toward the ranch. No sign of Jasper's folks or my pa coming after us. No neighbors who might tell that they'd seen us riding this way instead of toward the river, where we said we'd be.

"I'll feel better when we get off the main roads and

out of sight," I said. "Anybody we know could drive by and see us out here."

I scanned the road behind us for the umpteenth time. "Uh oh!"

"¿Qué pasó?" Jasper asked.

"Somebody's coming."

We pulled up the horses and swiveled around in our saddles. "Not the folks, though," I said.

A low black shape moved up the center of the road behind us, getting bigger as it moved closer. Was it a car? Someone on horseback? We both squinted into the growing light.

It wasn't a car or a horse. It was Willie!

He walked along with his nose to the ground, the old blind dog following our horses' scent trail down the road.

"Willie!" Jasper cried and the dog raised his head, grinning, like "Oh, there you are!" He trotted to catch up.

Jasper swung down, which made me nervous. I scanned the road in both directions. If a neighbor heading early to town drove by and saw us. . . .

Jasper hugged him while Willie sat on his big rump and wagged his tail. Tigger touched noses with Willie; the little family reunited.

"I guess he got out of his pen somehow," Jasper said, biting his lip and rubbing his dog's ear. "Are you mad at him?" He glanced up at me, his forehead wrinkled.

I considered it for a few seconds and shook my head. "It's too late to take him back; we'd get caught for sure."

"So he's coming?" Jasper smiled, his voice hopeful.

I let out a puff of breath. What choice did we have? Take him back and chance getting caught or bring him along and hope for the best?

"I reckon he is." Sometimes a thing gets decided for you and you just have to deal with it as best you can.

As if reading my thoughts, Jasper reminded me, "Willie's a hero, remember? He tracked down that lost little girl. He's brave and strong. He won't hold us back."

"True," I agreed, "he's a genuine hero, all right." That was even another story. "Keep a good eye on him, though." I nudged Rowdy with my heels and turned him back toward the mountains waiting for us.

Soon we left the paved road, the two-lane "highway," and started up the gravel road. I got down and opened the wire gate to skirt a cattle guard, waited while Jasper and Tig and Willie passed through, and hooked it back closed.

The horses' hooves crunched in the gravel. I was relieved to be out of sight of the main road, but my stomach quivered a little. We were getting farther and farther from help, if we needed it.

I shoved the nervousness down, everything was fine. No need to borrow trouble, as my pa says. Except for the addition of the dog, things were looking good so far. The weather was holding. No rain or snow in sight, but this time of year, storms sometimes rushed in and blackened the bluest skies.

Jasper and I didn't talk much, each of us swimming round in our own thoughts. Even the horses kept quiet, like they were lost in thought, too.

We rode abreast on the gravel road, just scrunch, scrunch, scrunch of the horses' hooves and the coyotes yipping good-bye to the night and the meadowlarks singing. We had a plan. We were on a mission. It was perfect.

We rode on for an hour or so, then turned off the gravel onto a rutted dirt road that wound steeper up through the sage and juniper stands.

Willie followed right along at Tigger's heel. Maybe he wouldn't be so much trouble after all. Maybe it would all go smooth and easy. Find the herd, turn them toward home. Follow them back. Me and Jasper are heroes. No problem.

Maybe.

Maybe not.

Chapter 6

As we rode farther into the mountains, my doubts lifted up with the rising sun and I felt free. No parents. No school. Nothing but us and our horses and dog. The deer and the coyotes knew that freedom, never knew anything else.

"What if we just keep going?" I said.

"What do you mean?" Jasper rode Tigger in the old wagon rut next to me and Rowdy.

"We could live off the land; build a shelter, hunt and fish, like the mountain men."

He was silent. After awhile he shook his head. "Someday. But right now, I couldn't hurt my folks like that."

Jasper's parents were nice. He loved them. And we were still kids. "I know. Just thinking out loud. Maybe someday."

"We should be almost to the gold mine," he said, changing the subject and, like before, his eyes glittered and his voice brightened when he said the word "gold."

Years ago, this road we were on had carried miners up to dig and wash tons of gravel, pounds of dirt looking for that sparkle. Then it took them, either smiling rich, hauling bags of gold, or poor and tired back down to the town below.

Seemed like I could feel them here, those folks taking a chance on fortune; everything at stake, leaving home and family, maybe a last-ditch try at making things right. Like us.

"See, if we found gold, we'd never have another problem," Jasper said. "We could buy anything we want, travel all over the world, own the biggest cattle ranch in the west. Can't you see it, Cass?"

"You're dreaming," I said. "Mrs. B. said only a few of those miners ever struck it rich. Most of them went home poorer than ever."

"But I have a feeling for it, almost like I could smell it out. I felt it on that field trip. If I could have stayed longer, I know I'd have found more than just that flake."

"Hmm. . . . Maybe." I let it go.

The track followed a wide, flat, dry streambed up a canyon that narrowed as it snaked up into the mountains.

Piles of tailings, mounds of gravel dredged up from the creek, lined the old creek bed. Like most mines in this country, gold was chased after both deep in the hills and in the creeks and riverbeds.

We passed through a gap between fence posts, the gray weathered gate slumped open in the sage, a robin gripping the splintered wood. The track widened out into a clearing, flat and open, surrounded by the skeletons and carcasses of fallen buildings: a line of miners' shacks, the overhung porch of the company store slumping into the dirt, an outhouse tilted but still standing. The remnants of the old Black Snake mining town.

"Need to use the toilet?" I joked, pointing at the dilapidated privy.

"Yeah, right," he said. "And get my butt snake-bit, no, gracias. But I could use a break."

I didn't want to stop for fear of never getting Jasper away from his hunt for riches. Still, I wasn't the boss. And he was helping me. I swung down and tied Rowdy off to an old hitching post in front of one of the fallen buildings.

"This was probably the bank where the miners got their gold weighed," I said. "Look at the stone walls and how thick the door is. I guess that was to stop robbers from getting in." I pulled hard at the rusty door handle, but nothing moved.

Jasper dismounted and tied Tig beside Rowdy.

"I'm going to look around, maybe find me a big gold nugget," Jasper said. He disappeared between the slumping shacks.

Great, I thought. There he goes. We should have just kept right on riding. Now the gold was calling him: "Look for me! Get rich! No more troubles." Just what the gold had whispered to all those miners years ago.

I shrugged and hoped he'd be back soon. I was digging around in my saddlebag for something to eat when a movement flashed in the corner of my eye, a shadow-shape skimming between buildings. Rowdy's head snapped up, his ears swiveled, and he stared at the spot where I'd seen the shape.

"Easy, boy. Probably just Jasper trying to spook us."

I moved to my horse's head and stroked his neck, still watching the gap between buildings, my heart beating fast.

The shadow-shape leaned out from the building and disappeared again. Rowdy snorted, his nostrils flaring, trying to catch the scent.

"So you saw it too, eh, Rowdy." I tried to sound soothing, unconcerned so as not to spook him further. Now Tig stiffened and snorted into the warm air. She backed up hard against her reins tied to the rail.

I moved between the two horses, held on to their reins just below their chins. "Easy, easy," I said softly, then, a little louder, "hey, Jasper, is that you?"

No answer. The horses danced in the dust. I untied their reins and held tight as I turned and walked them a few paces back. They twisted around to keep their eyes on the gap. There it was again: something, someone? darted across the space between the ramshackle buildings.

"Jasper!" I shouted.

"What?" I jumped at his voice just behind me.

"Take your horse," I said, handing him Tig's reins.

"¿Qué pasó!?" he said. "What's the matter with you? Seen a ghost?"

"Yeah. Maybe." I pointed to the space between the buildings: "There's someone here."

He peered into the shadows.

"Mount up," I whispered. "Let's get out of here." The hair on the back of my neck itched, like I'd crawled through a willow stand full of ticks.

A rattle like a boot kicking a tin can came from behind the old storefront.

Jasper jumped at the sound. "Vámonos, Cassie!"

We both swung into our saddles and turned the nervous horses toward the road that left the ghost town and headed up into the hills.

The horses danced a few steps, snorting and tossing their heads. We both kept our reins short and our legs tight to the horses' sides.

Suddenly, a terrible growling and snarling started up behind the old store.

"Willie!" Jasper and I shouted at once.

Then cuss words came flying out of the ruckus.

Jasper wheeled Tigger around. He squeezed her sides and she leaped through the gap between the buildings. Jasper reined her hard to the right and disappeared behind the store.

I followed. What else could I do?

Chapter 7

Rowdy and I bounded through the gap between the rickety old buildings. What a mess! Dust and arms and legs and teeth and tail all tangled and flying this way and that. Out of the snarling, swearing knot, an arm waved a rifle in the air. My heart bumped into high speed.

"Get this dog offa me!" a shrill voice rose out of the dust. Not a man's voice, but a woman's.

Willie had her pant leg in his teeth, shaking his head back and forth. The woman scrambled in the dirt, dropped the rifle, and grabbed her leg in her hands, trying to pull it away from Willie. Her gray hair flew loose and wild like a storm around her head.

Still in the saddle, Jasper shook out a loop on his rope and swung it in an easy circle over his head, calculating distance and timing like he was roping a calf.

Willie dragged the woman by her leg until she sat a few feet from where the rifle lay in the dirt. She shouted something I didn't catch over Willie's snarling, her voice raspy as a rusty hinge. She kicked at Willie with her free boot but missed.

Jasper's loop sailed through the air and settled neatly around the woman's shoulders, pinning her arms to her sides.

I jumped down off Rowdy and grabbed the gun. No way was I going to point it at an old lady. I slung it off into the sagebrush. My hands shook and my legs jellied.

"Good boy, Willie, let go," I said. The woman didn't look so dangerous unarmed and sitting in the dirt. But Willie clenched his teeth tighter on her pant leg and shook his head back and forth, growling like he'd brought down a grizzly.

Jasper tied the rope to his saddle horn and Tig backed up, pulling it tight between her and the woman on the other end of the rope, just like the good cow horse she was.

Jasper swung down. He grabbed Willie's collar. "¡No lo hagas, Willie, es suficiente!" Willie growled once more, then released the torn denim and backed off. He wagged his tail, looking pleased with himself.

"Let me go you little. . . ." The woman struggled to free herself from Jasper's rope.

"Why should we?" my voice shook. "Looks like you were going to shoot us!"

"I'm just protecting my gold," she snarled through yellow teeth. "Person's got a right to protect her property from thieves."

"Gold?" Jasper echoed the word like it was a magic spell.

"That's right, gold. My gold. Now let me go."

"I don't think she can hurt us without her gun," I said. "There's two of us. And Willie. Let her go."

Jasper untied the rope from his saddle horn and walked it down, coiling it in his hand as he went. He shook the loop bigger and snaked it loose over the woman's head.

"We're not after your gold," I said, "if there actually is any. We're just passing through. Going to get our cows down from the mountains."

"You really a gold miner?" Jasper asked. "Is there still gold here?"

I shot Jasper a look. I didn't like where this was going. "Like I said, we're not after gold, we're after cattle. Come on, Jasper, we need all the daylight we have to find the cattle."

The woman stood and slapped dust from her ratty button-down shirt and holey jeans. "Cattle, ha!" she scoffed. She looked Jasper up and down. "You've got the fever, don't you?" she said. "I smell it on you; I feel it."

I glanced from one to the other. Jasper stared into her eyes like he was in a trance. I bumped him with my elbow and tried to turn things around.

"You live up here?" I asked.

The woman spit on the ground and hobbled a few steps closer to where I'd thrown her rifle. "'Course I live here. Where else would I live?"

She scanned the sagebrush, looking for the rifle, but didn't seem to find it. "Can I get my gun back now?" she asked.

"Guess so," I said. Jasper nodded. I wasn't afraid of her now; just worried that she'd somehow snatch Jasper away from me.

I picked the gun out of the sage clump and handed it to her. She cracked it and sighted down the barrel. "You better not have busted my rifle."

"You shouldn't ought to point it at innocent people," Jasper said.

"Looks okay," she grumbled. "Need this for squirrels and rabbits. Don't shoot straight, what am I going to eat?"

We all stood there for a minute looking at each other.

I did appreciate that she hadn't said one word about Jasper and me just being kids on our own. She wasn't nice by a long shot, but at least she was talking to us like we were grown-ups. And she was living on her own up here, like I'd been daydreaming about.

Finally, Jasper said, "Sorry for my dog tearing your pants and for roping you."

She patted her head with both hands. She felt down one arm and then the other. "No harm done, I suppose." She squinted at us with her gray-blue eyes. "Now who did you say you were again?"

I stepped up. My pa had taught me to respect my elders and not to judge by appearances, so I offered up my hand. "I'm Cassie, this is Jasper, and the dog is Willie." Willie wagged his tail, like he hadn't been ready to chew the woman up about two minutes ago.

The old lady put out a hand. It felt light and bony as a bird when I held it for a second while we shook. "Elsinore," she said. "Call me Ellie."

Jasper stepped forward and said, "Pleased to meet you, ma'am," like he was being introduced to a friend of his folks after church. "So," he just couldn't let it go, "is there any gold left here?"

"What do I look like, an idiot?" The old woman spit in the dust again and wiped her hand across her mouth. "Think I'm living here for the scenery?"

"Can I see it?" Jasper asked, his eyes wide and bright. "Can I see the gold?"

I caught his eye, shook my head quick. If we got stalled out here with this crazy miner, we might not find the cattle before dark.

But Jasper shrugged, like he couldn't help himself and followed the woman toward the row of shabby cabins. Willie trailed behind, nose to the ground. I picked up both horses' reins and followed, leading them.

Instead of going into one of the shacks, though, the woman hobbled between two of them and up a short path to the foot of a hill that bounded the fallen town. I led the horses and Jasper walked close behind Ellie.

Jasper and I and Willie and the horses stopped behind her. She parted a big clump of bitterbrush and revealed a hole in the hillside, a doorway into the hill, into the mine. An adit I think Mrs. B. called it on the field trip.

Ellie cackled. "Is there gold here?" She could have been talking to us or to herself. "Heh-heh-heh! Gold? Yes indeed. Piles of it! Mounds of it! Buckets of it!" She turned to Jasper. "Bucket! Go get me a bucket!"

"What?" He turned around, searching. She gave him a shove back toward the buildings.

"Go, boy! Bring me a bucket for the gold."

Jasper darted off before I could stop him. Would we ever get out of here? And now I was alone with crazy Ellie. Come back, Jasper. I looked over my shoulder anxiously, but didn't want to turn my back on her.

Finally, Jasper reappeared gripping the broken handle of a rusted tin bucket.

"Good, good!" Ellie snickered. She turned her attention back to the adit.

Heavy juniper beams framed the mine entrance. Jasper's mouth hung open as he stepped closer and peered into the darkness. I hung back, still holding the horses. Willie stood at Jasper's side and sniffed the cold dark air coming up out of the mine.

"The shaft's narrow," Ellie said. "Gets smaller and tighter the deeper it goes."

She looked Jasper up and down, her watery eyes assessing him like a cow at auction. "Little wiry fella like you could get way down deep in there, bring up gold I can't get to."

I shook my head again, though Jasper didn't look at me. He only peered harder into the hole, like he was trying to draw the glinting gold out of the darkness. He stepped forward and bent down, looking deeper.

"Um, thanks, Ms. . . . um, thanks, Ellie," I stammered, "but we have to go. The cattle. Come on, Jasper." I tried to hand him Tigger's reins.

He leaned farther into the yawning mouth of the mine. Ellie stepped in close behind him, nearly breathing down his neck.

"Can you see it, boy?" she asked. "Can you see it shining down in there? I hear it calling your name, Jasper. I'll share everything you bring up, bucket after bucket." She nudged his back until he took a small step into the blackened doorway.

"I think I see it!" Jasper cried, taking another step in, squinting into the black tunnel.

"Go a little deeper." Ellie prodded his shoulder. "See it?" Jasper took a few more steps into the darkness. I could barely see his back now.

All at once, a cold fear grabbed me. "No, Jasper!" I stepped up behind them, pushing the old woman aside. She shrieked and gripped Jasper's arm.

"Help me, boy! Help me get the gold!!" She said it so pitifully, I almost gave in.

"No." I shook my head and pulled my friend out of her grasp. "Jasper, let's go!" We stumbled backwards, out of the dark mine and into the blazing daylight.

"But, the gold!" he said. "Think of all the cattle we could buy, a whole ranch! I'll just go down for a minute. We know where the herd is. It won't take any time at all to find them."

Jasper's eyes were fever bright. "Just for a minute, Cassie!" he begged. "Please!"

I handed him Tig's reins. "No."

Ellie staggered toward us, reaching out for Jasper like he was a life preserver and she was sinking.

"We're going," I repeated. I grabbed Jasper's shoulders and stared him in the eyes. I shook him, trying to bring him back to his senses. "Forget the gold, Jasper. There isn't any. We're going to get the cattle, just like we said we would. To save the ranch. Remember our plan?"

Ellie stopped. Her hands fell to her sides. Jasper blinked and shook his head, like he was waking up out of a dream. He held Tigger's reins and stepped to her side.

Jasper swung into the saddle. I mounted and turned Rowdy and started him up the road away from the mine.

When I looked back, Jasper was following me, but his head hung down. Willie trailed behind.

I heard Ellie calling out behind us, "Hey, boy! Be sure you come back and help me get this gold out, eh? You come back anytime."

Chapter 8

We rode without talking. Jasper and Tigger followed a few yards behind me and Rowdy. I couldn't tell if my friend was mad that I'd taken him from his gold or embarrassed at having almost fallen for the old woman's trap.

The road dwindled into a double dirt track and then into a single trail. Juniper and sage gave way to pine and fir trees. The forest grew thicker. Ice age boulders rested among the trees on the hillsides. I felt like we were riding through a dark old story, some ancient lore with hidden meanings.

We skirted fallen logs and piles of rocks. The trail hadn't been traveled or kept up much at all.

"After we get the cattle home," I offered, "we can go back and look for the gold, if you want, that is."

Nothing.

"Jasper," I tried again. "You mad at me?"

No answer.

"Guess that's a yes." I shrugged. Couldn't be helped; we barely had enough time for the job in front of us as it was. I hoped Jasper's hurt feelings would blow over. "You know I couldn't do this without you, right?"

"Mm-hmm."

"So, thanks."

I heard a sigh behind me, over the clip-clop of the horses' hooves on gravel.

"Para servirle."

I smiled and clucked Rowdy into a trot. Everything would get back on track.

"Must be close to noon," I said. The sun was nearly straight overhead, cutting down on us between the tree boughs.

The air chilled as we rode higher into the forested mountains. The coyote willow in the gullies was gold and the dogwood orange, like we were riding into another, colder season.

A cold wind sifted through the trees. I pulled my cowboy hat down low and my shirt collar up.

Jasper sang a low, slow Spanish song behind me: "De la Sierra Morena, cielito lindo, vienen bajando, un par de ojitos negros, cielito lindo, de contrabando."

I liked the way it floated through the autumn air. I pretended we were on a bigger journey, maybe up to Canada, maybe down to Mexico.

Up ahead, a huge dark lump of something sat smack in the middle of the trail. Rowdy snorted and sidestepped as we got nearer. Willie growled and sniffed around the edge. Horse manure. Lots of it.

Jasper came up beside us. "What the heck is that doing here?"

"Stud pile," I said. "Wild stallions leave them to mark their territory."

"Wild horses? Up here in the woods?"

"Yeah," I said, "ferals and their offspring from the early settlers and miners and people nowadays who just can't feed their stock. They let them go and they join the wild herds. Pa told me about them."

Both horses danced a circle around the pile, sniffing it suspiciously. "Keep an eye out for them," I warned. "A wild stallion might not like strange horses in his territory. He could spook Rowdy and Tig or even try to fight them."

"Why don't the wild horses go down low to the pastures and fields? Why stay up here in the woods?" Jasper held Tig's reins low and patted her neck to calm her.

"Safety, I guess. Horses are prey animals. People are predators. No people up here. The horses come down in the winter, when they have to, when there's no grass left in the high meadows. Ranchers won't tolerate them in their fields, though, eating their winter pasture and their hay stacks."

Willie started to lean into the pile with his shoulder.

"No, Willie!" Jasper shouted. "¡No entres a lo que huele mal!" Willie jumped up and gave the pile another deep snuffle. "I don't want a poop-stinking dog near my sleeping bag tonight," Jasper laughed.

"I don't know," I said, laughing now, too. "Might smell better than you after a day in the saddle."

We skirted the pile and went on up the trail. Willie followed, turning to sniff behind us, probably bewildered that we didn't want to roll in the stinking heap alongside him.

I thought about the horses up here when the weather turned bitter and the food disappeared under the snow. The stallions would lead them down and they'd take their chances with the ranchers. Some would starve. Some would be rounded up and auctioned off. Some would be shot.

It wasn't their fault they were here. Just another one of life's unfairnesses that stung me.

Jasper started up singing again behind me.

I scanned the ground for tracks from our cattle. I wasn't going to tell Jasper, but I didn't really recognize this draw we were riding up. I hoped we would find some sign of the herd soon. Or something I recognized, at least. I hoped we would have the herd corralled up in a nice safe canyon for the night, ready to head home in the morning.

Jasper's singing stopped suddenly. He'd pulled Tig to a halt.

"Psst! Cass!" he whispered. "What was that?"

I started to say that I didn't hear anything, but then I did—a snort and a rustle in the willows to our right. Rowdy jumped sideways and swung his head toward the noise.

"Cripes! I don't—" The rustle turned into a crashing as the willows bent and parted.

A big black horse pounded out of the trees. He was taller and broader than Rowdy, sleek and muscular with a long tangled mane and tail. He snorted and reared up, slashing the air between us with his hooves.

Behind him, half a dozen horses appeared out of the shrubs, his band of mares.

Rowdy backed up. I shortened the reins and wrapped my legs tight around him. I grabbed the saddle horn with one hand. "Whoa . . . easy, boy," I soothed.

The stallion neighed shrill and loud like he needed to reach the far end of the mountain range.

Next thing I knew, Tigger was rearing up and backing away at the same time and Jasper was on the ground, trying desperately to keep hold of his horse's reins. Willie barked and growled but stayed behind Tigger.

I hung on tight as Rowdy danced and circled and whinnied at Tigger.

The stallion circled Tigger and Jasper, his hooves coming closer and closer to them. He nudged Tig with his nose and turned his hind end toward Jasper, bucking and kicking.

"He wants Tig!" Jasper shouted from where he'd landed in the dirt.

Jasper rolled aside and jumped to his feet, still holding Tig's reins in one hand. With the other hand, he swatted at the stallion with his hat.

"No!" he yelled, "get away! You can't have her!"

I nudged Rowdy forward and started yelling too, waving my arms. Willie advanced, barking like a Doberman guarding a junkyard, all bared teeth and bristled back.

I guess all of us together were too much for him. The stallion whinnied and wheeled around, then crashed back into the willows.

We watched as the black horse galloped up the far bank and through the pines and scrub oak and boulders with his band of mares. Then they were gone, disappeared like ghosts, lost in the thickening trees.

"You okay?" I swung down next to Jasper who stood and batted the dirt from his butt. He stroked Tigger's neck with a trembling hand.

"Yeah, but that was close, huh, Tig?"

We sat on a big rock and I pulled out a water bottle and we both drank deep. We sat until the horses calmed and started nibbling the bunchgrass and our hearts stopped thundering in our chests.

No sign of the stallion coming back. I scanned the hilltops and the trees. Then I kicked around in the dirt at my feet.

"Look," I said, "cattle tracks!"

There in the dust among all the hoofprints and our boot tracks were the round split tracks of cows.

"Has to be our herd." I followed them with my eyes. "They're headed south up that gully."

Jasper smiled. "If it wasn't for that stallion, we might've gone the wrong way."

We mounted up and headed after the cattle. I hoped that was the last of our troubles.

No such luck.

Chapter 9

We came out of the trees and the trail ended. Just ended right at the banks of the Little Copper River. A low dip in the bank with the grass worn away showed where the cattle had forded the river.

I led the way. Rowdy is good at river crossings. He waded right in. The water only reached his knees at its deepest. He picked his way among the cobbles on the riverbed. The water was so shallow and clear, I could see the small pebbles and a trout darting between Rowdy's feet. He crunched up onto the gravel bar and loped up the bank.

Jasper urged Tigger forward and she dipped a hoof in and stepped back. I laughed and Jasper glared at me. He urged her forward and she crossed in big leaps and ran up the bank next to where I sat on Rowdy.

"She's not made too many river crossings," Jasper said by way of excuse. "Good girl, Tig." He patted her neck.

A river crossing can be treacherous for a horse when the water's deep and the footing's rough. They are naturally cautious animals and a rider has to give them confidence.

We watched as Willie sniffed the water's edge, lapped up a long drink of cold water, and stood on the bank with his nose in the air.

"¡Ven acá, Willie! ¡Estamos aquí!" Jasper shouted to his blind dog. To me he said, "He's lost our scent in the water."

I hoped this wasn't going to be the beginning of problems with having a blind old dog tagging along.

Willie perked up his ears at Jasper's voice and waded across to us.

Like he was reading my mind, Jasper said, "See, no problem."

I smiled, hoping he was right.

The trail started rising steeply after the river crossing. The air had a bite now. The horses huffed up the switchbacks and we rested them more often.

Boulders rested among the pines and firs, left there by glaciers long ago. Rocky cliffs edged the hilltops. A red-tailed hawk screeched along the rimrock. The country grew more rugged, like it was trying to throw us back down to the valley where we belonged.

We climbed up into winter. Snow-colored clouds ate the blue autumn sky.

"It's getting colder." I watched my breath turn to fog and float out over Rowdy's mane.

"Yep." Jasper's voice came muffled through his bandana, which he'd pulled up over his nose.

My leather gloves had stiffened up and I flexed my fingers out from the reins, trying to limber them up.

"¡Hace mucho frío! I can't feel my toes," Jasper mumbled.

"Pull your feet out of the stirrups and swing them to get the blood moving," I said.

Last thing I needed was to bring Jasper back to the ranch with a couple of toes missing from frostbite.

"Wish I had some of those woolly chaps, or the ones with the cow hair still on 'em. Or those tapaderas that cover your toes in your stirrups."

Jasper and I were both just wearing jeans, flannel shirts, wool blanket coats, and cowboy boots. "Sorry, Jas. I should have thought to dress warmer. Who would have thought it was already winter up here?"

He trotted up even with me. I could hear the cold shiver in his voice. "Think we'll find the cattle soon?"

"Sure. Real soon."

I pulled Rowdy to a halt in a small clearing where the pines thinned out. We'd been following the cattle tracks up the trail for what felt like hours. I thudded down out of the saddle, knowing I'd have to pull myself back up.

"This cow pie is still pretty soft," I said, poking a squashed green pile of droppings with a stick. "Not steaming warm, but not frozen or dried out. So I'd say they're only an hour or so ahead."

"Wonder why they're heading uphill instead of down," Jasper said. "Doesn't make sense to go where it's colder and there's less food."

I scanned the ground some more, turning around in the clearing. "I think I know." I pointed with the cow pie poking stick. "Look. Horse tracks. And they're wearing horseshoes, so they're not wild."

Jasper dismounted and hunkered down beside me. "Someone's herding our cows up into the mountains?"

I nodded. "Looks that way. If they *are* our cows. If not, then someone else is trespassing on our allotment."

Our ranch, like a lot of them down in the river valley, had summer grazing permits in the mountains. Letting your cattle or sheep graze on someone else's allotment was like stealing.

"What're we going to do?" Jasper took his black felt hat off and ran his fingers through his hair, moving from one foot to the other like he was nervous.

I shrugged. "Follow them, I guess."

"Really? If they're stealing the herd, that makes them cattle rustlers, just like in the old movies." Jasper was wide-eyed now.

"Cows are worth a lot of money. People will steal them just like anything else," I said.

"What'll we do if we catch them?" Jasper looked as excited as he'd been at the gold mine, but scared now, too. "Maybe we should go back and get help."

I thought it over for about two seconds. "That would ruin everything," I said, still picturing us as the returning heroes. "Besides, who's going to come? We couldn't find anyone to help bring the cattle down in the first place."

I tried to sound confident. "We'll keep an eye out; see the rustlers before they see us. They won't be expecting anyone to be following them up here. We'll figure out how to get the cows back when the time comes."

I hoisted myself back into the saddle with a grunt. A twinge in my gut told me that our troubles were only beginning. We headed onward, higher and deeper into the mountains, chasing our herd of cattle.

And chasing whoever had them.

Chapter 10

The trail grew steeper and rockier. A few flakes of snow drifted down. The horses stumbled and their heads hung down. My legs and back ached. Jasper looked miserable; head low, body slumped over his saddle horn, reins held slack. Willie dragged along behind, limping and footsore.

"Can we stop for a bit? Willie's tired." Jasper and Tig paused to let the old dog catch up.

The snow was settling on the trail; the temperature had dropped below freezing. Dusky shade gathered between the trees. It was getting late, probably five or even six, by the low sun and long shadows.

"Maybe we better make camp and catch up with the cows in the morning," I said.

No answer from Jasper. That wasn't good. I led our

little troop up over the crest of the next hill, where the land flattened out and the trees thinned and I could see a fair ways. Not a cow in sight.

Should I make use of the last hour or so of daylight to push us on a few more miles? If the rustlers still had the herd on the move, they'd be even farther away in the morning. It was a choice even a grown-up would have trouble with.

"Jasper. We're making camp." I was responsible for us being up here. I was going to make sure we all got back down.

I chose a grove of pine trees sheltered by a rock outcropping. Nearby, a rickety split-rail fence enclosed a clump of aspens. The grass within was green and lush: a spring. Fresh water.

I dismounted and led Rowdy to the pines and tied him to a low branch. Jasper practically fell out of the saddle; he was that cold and tired. I knew I'd made the right choice to stop. Willie collapsed in the soft pine needles under the hanging boughs.

"Lo siento, Willie," Jasper's voice shook as he knelt by his dog. "I should have taken you back home when I could've."

"He'll be okay. He just needs a good night's rest." I hoped it was true. Willie was old, after all, and he'd had a hard life before Jasper got him from the shelter. I handed Jasper my coat. "Put this over him," I said.

I trudged through the tall dry grass now dusted with snow to check on the spring. Ranchers had fenced it in to keep the cattle and deer from muddying it up. A pipe led from the spring to a metal trough green with moss and algae. A skim of ice hardened the surface of the water. I broke it with a juniper branch.

I led both horses over and let them have a good long drink. Rowdy blew bubbles in the icy water. I brought the horses back to the grove.

"Water comes straight from the spring," I said. "We can drink it, too, and refill our water bottles."

Unless you saw the water coming right out of the ground, it really wasn't a good idea to drink out of a stream or river anymore: I'd heard of too many cases of "beaver fever" from dirty water, people sick with the runs for days or even weeks. That was a trouble we sure didn't need up here.

I unhooked Rowdy's cinch and pulled his saddle and pad off. I traded his bridle for the halter I'd brought. I tied a line between two trees and tied the lead rope in a loop so it could slide back and forth on the line and clipped the lead to Rowdy's halter.

Jasper climbed to his feet, unsaddled Tigger, and

tied her likewise. He brought Willie a tin cup full of water from the spring and the old dog lapped the cup dry. Jasper refilled it from his water bottle and the dog drank that too.

The horses nibbled at the snowy bunchgrass. I poured some oats onto the ground in front of each horse and they lipped it off the snowy dirt.

Jasper rooted through the saddlebags until he came up with some jerky. He leaned back on an elbow next to Willie and tore off pieces and fed them to the dog.

"You eat some of that, too," I said. "And how about passing me some?"

He grinned, seeming to snap out of his discomfort a little and threw me a hunk of dried meat.

I tore off a bite. We sat and chewed in silence for a few minutes. The wind picked up, setting the aspen leaves shivering and whispering. The vast high plain spread out around us, mountains shifting green to dark blue on the horizon. The cloudy sky hung low and soft and gray and cold.

"Ever hear this much quiet before?" Jasper asked. "I mean, the wind in the grass, nothing else?"

"All I hear is you gnawing that jerky," I said, tossing a pinecone at him. Now that I'd eaten, I felt a giddy kind of exhaustion, wired up and wrung out at the same time.

"Feeling better?" I asked.

"Yeah."

Jasper threw a pinecone back, hitting me in the shoulder. I threw one back and missed. War broke out: Jasper let out a whoop and hefted a flat, dried cow pie at me like a Frisbee.

"Shhhh!" I hissed, ducking: "The rustlers might hear you!"

Willie was on his feet, barking and chasing us.

"Shhh, Willie!" I stopped and rested with my hands on my thighs. "We better be quiet before we give ourselves away."

Jasper and I collapsed under the pines and lay on our backs, breathing hard.

"See what some jerky and water will do for you?" I puffed.

"Yep. I'm a new man."

I stared up at the endless sky, feeling happy, free, and peaceful. "You know, even if something really bad happens and we don't bring back the cattle and save the ranch," I said, "I'm still glad we came."

"Me too." Jasper nodded and pulled Willie to him in the pine needles and they play wrestled gently, Willie snapping at the air and Jasper tickling the big dog's belly.

I watched the horses grazing and a hawk or eagle,

too high to tell which, soar through the gently falling snow. The mountain range faded off, peak after peak, ghostly in their snowy robes. This was my home; I belonged here as sure as that soaring bird.

Hard as the day had been, and hard as things may be to come, I knew how lucky I was. And I felt more certain than ever that I'd shrivel up and die if Pa made us move to the city.

Rustlers or no rustlers, we had to get the cattle back and bring them home.

Chapter 11

We lay on our backs for a good half hour, eating pemmican and dried fruit and more jerky. My stomach was full and my hands and feet had thawed out. Jasper lay with his head on Willie's stomach, looking up at the sky, too.

The wind blew the sky clear and a few stars glimmered silver as darkness came on.

"Funny to think those stars have been up there all day and we just couldn't see them," I said.

"You're a philosopher, now?" Jasper asked. "Or maybe an astronomer?"

"No. I'm just saying."

Jasper and I untied our sleeping bags from behind our saddles and unrolled them under the pine boughs, close to the trunk where the ground was dry and the needles piled deepest. I hauled my saddle over to use as a pillow and Jasper rolled up his coat.

I was leaning on one elbow, half under my blanket when I saw it: a pinpoint of light far out across the plateau. I sat up.

"Jas. . . . Look!"

"¿Qué es eso?" He sat up beside me. "A campfire!"

"Yep. Has to be the cattle thieves," I said. "Who else would be up here?"

"Wonder where they've got the herd put up."

"Probably made a brush fence and penned them up in some little canyon."

I slung off my blankets and pulled on my boots. "Well? What are you waiting for? Let's go get our cows back."

Jasper was on his feet in a minute, shoving his arms through his coat sleeves. Willie had jumped up, too, probably catching our excitement.

"We better go on foot and leave the horses and Willie here until we've checked things out." I didn't want Willie getting hurt or the smell of our horses spooking their horses.

"Lo siento, Willie." Jasper tied the dog to the pine tree trunk with a lead rope. "Tú estás encargado del lugar y necesitas cuidar muy bien, mi amigo." Willie whined softly, lay down, and rested his chin on his paws.

I grabbed a flashlight from the saddlebag, but didn't turn it on. The stars and the rising half-moon were bright enough to see the bunchgrass clumps and rocks and sagebrush. We started across the plateau toward the firelight.

I led the way. Jasper kept close behind me. He was so quiet, so light on his feet, even with his bad leg, I wouldn't have known he was there.

We crept along for a quarter mile or so. When I could see the fire clearly and the shapes of men hunkered around it, I stopped. Jasper bumped up close behind me.

"Listen. . . ." I whispered.

Cows mooing softly. Close to the fire, low voices and laughter. We ducked behind a tall clump of sage. I held my breath. Someone stood and stretched, a tall silhouette against the firelight.

"I think there's three," Jasper said. "That one standing and two sitting."

"Yep."

"Three against two."

"Yep."

"And they're bigger. A lot."

"Shhh. . . ." I said. "Come on."

We circled around the camp, keeping low and moving fast and quiet.

The standing man stepped out of the firelight and into the darkness between us. We froze in our tracks. He was squinting into the darkness right at us. I held my breath, watching his dark shape, the fire shifting and sparking bright behind him.

Finally, he turned, walked back, and sat down on the ground by the fire.

I let out a slow breath. I motioned Jasper to follow and we went on around the camp, keeping far away, well clear of the firelight.

"Lucky they didn't bring dogs," Jasper whispered.

"Shhh. . . ." I put my finger to my lips. He was right. A herding dog would have caught our scent and barked his head off.

"Wonder where their horses are," Jasper whispered.

We ranged around in the dark, farther and farther from the campfire until we heard a soft nicker and the tearing of bunchgrass.

Behind a stand of junipers, maybe fifty yards or more from the men, three horses stood hobbled. The hobbles, cuffs around the horses' ankles connected by a short length of chain, let the horses graze and walk around without being able to run away.

Two were dark, maybe bays, and one was a paint, like Rowdy, his white patches shining bright in the darkness. They lifted their heads, all three at once, as we got close. One snorted and the murmured talk by the fire stopped.

"You hear something?" one of the men said.

"No. What?"

"Horse snorted. Caught cougar scent, maybe?"

"Nah. No cougar's gonna come this close to people and fire."

"I 'spose."

Silence. Then they picked up talking again. No one was coming to check on the horses. So far, we were lucky.

Jasper touched my arm and gestured to the right. A narrow gap in the rimrock was shuttered up with juniper limbs and pine branches: a makeshift fence. Behind it, corralled in the canyon, were the cattle, lowing and shuffling in the darkness.

"At least they're far enough from the camp that the guys probably won't wake up when we let them out," Jasper whispered, "at least not right away. Give us a head start."

I moved closer. I shined the flashlight through the brushy barrier. The beam flashed over the cows' dark sides and shone in the whites of their eyes. Blue ear tags on the cows; yellow on the calves. Our ranch's brand on their hips.

Up until then, I hadn't been certain. Now I was. My heart thudded in my chest. They were rustlers! And they had our herd! Anger surged up in me, hot and fierce.

"Yep," I nodded, trying to calm myself. "They're ours."

Jasper nodded and ducked his head, pointing with his chin that we should return to our own camp. We slipped off into the darkness. We knew all we needed to know.

Now it was time to take back what was ours. But how?

Chapter 12

We made our way back to camp by moonlight. Since the clouds had cleared off, the air was biting cold. I shivered and rubbed my icy fingers against my jeans.

Rowdy whinnied softly as we approached our camp. Willie whined as Jasper knelt and untied him. Jasper sat on the freezing ground close to the tree trunk, where the branches collected the snow, leaving bare spots underneath.

I forced myself to keep quiet. I wanted to shout and stomp around. I wanted to gallop back and ask those good-for-nothings what they thought they were doing with our cows. Instead, I paced in tight circles, my arms crossed firm over my chest. I kicked rocks and felt like steam was boiling out of my ears, I was that pent up.

Jasper watched me silently rage for a minute or two. He pulled a grass stem and chewed it where he sat in the dark in the dirt. He fingered the lucky horseshoe charm on the chain around his neck.

My heartbeat finally slowed and some of the anger gave way to frustration, then to puzzling it out. "Well," I asked, slumping down next to Jasper, "how should we go about this? Are we really going to get the herd back by ourselves, or should we go for help, now that we know the rustlers really have our cows?"

"While you've been stomping and shooting smoke out your ears," he said, "I've been making a plan."

"Ha-ha. You saying you're not mad at them?"

"'Course I'm mad," he said. "But being mad's not a plan. It won't get the herd back."

"Right. Let's hear it, then."

"First, we can do this ourselves. If we went for help, they'd be long gone before we got back. So, we wait."

"Wait? I'm not in a waiting mood." I was on my feet again, pacing.

"Listen. We wait until they're asleep, maybe just before dawn, so we have a bit of light. We split up outside their camp. One of us gets their horses out of there, far enough away that they can't just mount up and ride after us."

"How are we going to get the horses out of there without waking anybody up?"

"Very quietly."

"Yeah, well, I hope you tell that to the horses."

Jasper rolled his eyes.

"Okay," I said, "I'll lead the horses away, quiet as little mice. Then you open the brush fence and get the cattle out?"

"Right." He nodded. "You let the horses go, then come and help me with the cows. We'll drive them far enough off that we've got a good head start when the rustlers wake up and see the cows are gone."

I considered. "What about when they come after us?"

"Like you said before, we'll cross that bridge when we get there."

I swallowed hard. He was right. There was no time to get help. It was up to us.

Jasper leaned over and pulled some pemmican out of the saddlebag. He broke it in half and handed me a piece.

"I don't think I can sleep for thinking about it."

"Nope," Jasper said, "plus it's too cold to sleep."

We both leaned back on our bedrolls. I pictured the rustlers' camp; where they'd be sleeping, where the cattle were, the horses.

Over and over, I ran through the plan in my mind; letting their horses go, tearing down the brush gate, herding the cattle away.

I pictured all the things that could go wrong: their horses not running off or making too much noise and waking the rustlers up, the cattle scared and bawling and waking them up, Jasper or me tripping and falling in the dark, maybe twisting an ankle, and waking them up. The rustlers chasing us, maybe even shooting at us.

So many dangers to worry about. . . .

Then I woke up. When had I dropped off?

"Hey, Jasper! Wake up!" He was snoring next to me, his hat over his eyes.

"What?" He sat up and stretched. "Uh-oh. Guess I fell asleep after all."

"Yeah, me too." I stood. The sky was already starting to lighten to the east. I was stiff from cold. "Pack up, quick. We'll just have to hope they're not awake yet."

"My boots are frozen." Jasper rubbed and creased and folded the leather until he could jam his foot in. "Should have put them under the blankets."

We shoved everything into the saddlebags, chewing mouthfuls of jerky while we worked. My stomach felt tight and empty, like it was pressed up against my backbone. Flapjacks and eggs were starting to sound good.

We saddled the horses and strapped our sleeping bags behind our saddles. I had to keep blowing on my fingers and tucking them into my armpits to thaw them out. The horses snorted frosty clouds into the air.

"What about Willie?" Jasper was kneeling, stroking the dog's head while Willie gnawed his own piece of jerky.

I thought a minute. "We sure can't have him with us when we drive off their horses and let the cows out. He'd get trampled for sure. Or bark."

"He has to come," Jasper said, his voice sharp and strained. "We can't leave him here. There'll be no time to come back for him!"

I scanned the sky, which was getting lighter every minute. As my pa would say, we were burning daylight standing here.

"Okay," I conceded. "Just try to keep Willie close and quiet."

We mounted up and headed across the plain toward the rustlers' camp. This was it: either we succeeded and got our cows back and got away or we got caught by angry cattle thieves. . . .

Chapter 13

My heart beat hard and my breath came shallow and fast, the cold night air seeming to chill my lungs and burst back out. The horses walked slowly, picking their way among the rocks and scrub in the dark. I held the reins loosely and let Rowdy find his own way.

The moonlight made everything shadowy and strange. A shimmer of snow dusted the ground, shining like sand.

The embers of the rustlers' campfire glowed like eyes in the dark. Three dark shapes lay stretched near the coals. Good. They were all there.

I held my breath and reined Rowdy in a wide circle around the sleeping men. Luckily, there were enough junipers and bitterbrush scattered across the flats, we could stay pretty well hidden.

We stopped and I waved Jasper toward the right, in the direction of the little canyon where the cattle were penned up. He nodded and he and Tig faded into the darkness. Willie snuffled quietly along at Tigger's heel. So far, so good.

I came up from behind the camp to where the three horses were hobbled. They stood alert, nostrils flared, sniffing my scent and Rowdy's. I got down and tied Rowdy to a tree branch a few yards away.

"Tell them I mean them no harm," I whispered to Rowdy, because I know that horses speak to one another in ways we can't hear.

Rowdy stood calmly and pushed against my back with his nose. The horses stopped fidgeting and let me come close. The paint stepped toward me; little, slow steps because of the hobbles.

I stroked his nose, then bent and unstrapped the cuffs around his ankles, dropping them in the dirt. Then I moved to the other two and did the same. They milled around and then moved off onto the plain. Time to get them moving even farther.

I swung up into the saddle and rode toward them, swinging my rope. I moved slowly, walking Rowdy behind them, pushing them across the plain.

"Quiet, slow, quiet, slow," I whispered to myself.

"Easy Rowdy, easy now," I whispered.

When I felt like we were far enough away not to be heard, I squeezed Rowdy into a trot and came at them faster, swinging the rope in a loop above my head.

The rustlers' horses picked up a trot and then a canter and then a full gallop, tossing their heads and kicking up their heels at their freedom and good fortune. I felt like I'd done at least one good thing. When the horses were out of sight over the edge of the plain, I turned Rowdy back.

I let out a rush of breath I didn't know I'd been holding. Part One of the plan was a success! But how was Jasper doing?

When I got to the mouth of the canyon, Jasper and Tig were there, as promised. Jasper had torn away most of the brush that fenced the cattle in. Part Two was almost a success, too.

There was still no sound or movement from the sleeping bodies by the fire pit. Somebody or something was watching over us. Or maybe Jasper's lucky horseshoe charm had kicked in.

I hopped down and helped drag away the rest of the brush. Even Willie grabbed a branch in his mouth and hauled it to the side. The opening grew big enough for the cows to pass through. I could see their heavy shapes standing a few feet inside the canyon. I could smell their wet manure, musky and warm in the cold air.

The cattle, our cattle, stood there blinking in the thin morning light. None of them took a step. My heart beat fast and hard in my ribs. We couldn't afford to holler to get them moving. What if they wouldn't budge?

The darkness had turned from black to gray and the sky brightened to the east. We were running out of time. The men would wake up. . . .

"Come on cows, come on," I said under my breath. They looked at me, but didn't move toward the opening.

"I'll slip in behind them and get them going," I said. "Get ready to move them on when they come out."

Jasper mounted up. I led Rowdy off a few yards and tied him to a sagebrush clump.

I edged along the rock wall of the canyon. The cows moved their bodies between me and their calves, shuffling around in the dim light filtering into the canyon. I felt my way to the back wall of the little canyon and spread my arms and called quietly, "Here we go, girls, here we go, right on out."

Slowly they began to move in front of me, the calves sticking close to their mothers' sides. I hoped they didn't feel my nervousness and get jumpy themselves.

"That's it, nice and calm," I said. "Slow and easy, nice and quiet."

After a tense minute, the last cow and calf moved out of the canyon. When they were all out in the open, Jasper and Tigger moved in behind them. I untied Rowdy and mounted up.

Jasper swung his rope slowly over his head and the cattle moved as a group away from the camp and out across the plain. Jasper was a natural cowboy and the cows knew what he meant without him saying a thing. Willie followed Tigger. Rowdy and I came along behind.

Seeing our brand on their hips made me mad all over again, which overrode some of my fear. I was more determined than ever to get them home.

I moved alongside the herd, glancing again and again back at the camp. In the growing light, I thought I saw a shape moving around, maybe a man standing . . . but it was too far away to make out for sure. The hair on the back of my neck stood up.

"Hurry, Jasper," I hissed, "I think they're waking up!"

The cattle quickly fanned out across the plateau, Jasper behind them and me flanking them on the left, steering them toward the edge of the plain, back to the trail we'd come up the day before. They mooed low, but didn't bawl. It was almost like they knew it was important to keep quiet. Knew what we were trying to do.

We were about halfway across the open plain when I heard voices behind me. Then shouting. Then I hollered and Jasper hollered and we swung our ropes at the cows and drove them faster toward the edge of the plateau.

I didn't look back now, just kept going, but I could perfectly picture in my mind the three men discovering their horses were gone and the cattle were gone and trying to yank on their boots to chase after us on foot.

The cattle disappeared over the edge of the plateau and charged down the trail. I followed, feeling the protection of the forest close in around us. Jasper dropped down into the forest behind the last cow.

We'd done it!

The herd was heading down the trail. The rustlers were far behind (I hoped). If we could just keep the cows together and moving downhill, we'd be home by suppertime. Pa would be so happy and proud. I pictured his smile, him gathering me up in a big hug, shaking Jasper's hand. . . .

But we weren't there yet. Miles of rough country stretched between us and home: forest to lose cattle in, the cold air getting colder, and the rustlers coming after us.

Chapter 14

We didn't slow down or stop for a good hour, just kept the cattle moving through the trees, back down the narrow trail where we'd followed their hoofprints yesterday. Hard to believe that was only yesterday; seemed like weeks ago. I was exhausted from the riding and excitement and anger and hardly any sleep on the frozen ground.

Jasper rode behind the herd, keeping them moving down the trail. I went after strays, running them up out of creek beds and juniper stands. Both of us looked behind us time after time, expecting to see someone darting in between the trees, or just plain pursuing us, angry and dangerous. But no one showed.

The snow disappeared as we moved lower down

the mountain, like we'd gone from autumn to winter and back to autumn again.

The cattle were moving steadily now. Jasper rode up beside me. "Those rustlers have no clue they've been beaten by a couple of kids."

I grinned at him. I'd kind of forgotten we were only twelve. "Bet city kids couldn't get back a herd of cows from some rustlers."

"Probably couldn't even get on a horse."

"Or rope a calf."

"Or camp out on their own."

We rode on awhile. I thought about it. "It's not really their fault, though, is it?"

"What? Who?"

"Kids who grow up in the city. And they can probably do things we can't."

"Like what?"

"I don't know, play the tuba or dance ballet."

"Who wants to play the tuba?"

I sighed. "You're missing the point. But, right. Who'd rather play the tuba than ride a horse?"

We were both silent, pondering the city kid versus country kid idea when Rowdy suddenly jumped sideways, right out from underneath me.

Rowdy whinnied and snorted, pawing the air.

I landed on my butt in the dirt. I still held one rein, while Rowdy strained hard against my grip, tossing his head and backing up.

"Cass. . . . Don't move. . . ." Jasper said it calm and quick. "Rattlesnake."

I opened my mouth to say, "Don't be ridiculous, they're all hibernating," when I looked down. Coiled up about three feet from my right hand, hissing and rattling, was a fat gray-green diamondback rattler.

I froze.

"Don't jerk away. Move your hand real slowly," Jasper advised.

"Easy for you to say," I said through gritted teeth. I wanted nothing more than to jerk my hand and scramble away. But I knew he was right.

I let go of the reins and Rowdy took a few steps back. The snake raised its head up higher out of its coiled body, rattling louder.

My whole body tightened up. I held my breath and moved my hand slowly, slowly away from the snake.

The rattler looked long, five or six feet, and its fat body coiled tight. It had eaten a lot of mice to see it through the winter.

I got my shaking hand back near my body and began to inch my butt across the gravel, away from the snake. I hoped it couldn't hear my heart thundering like hoofbeats in a stampede.

Next thing I knew, nothing was going slow. It all happened in a flash of hooves and snake and flying rocks. Rowdy reared up and came crashing down hard on the rattler with his front hooves. The snake flew up from the impact and for a few seconds hung wrapped around Rowdy's leg.

I yelled and jumped out of the way of the flailing horse and snake.

Then the snake was back on the ground, under Rowdy's hooves, tattered and flat and oozing its innards out into the dirt. Thud, thud, thud, Rowdy came down hard on the snake over and over again. Finally, he backed off and stood blowing and trembling.

Jasper got down off Tigger and poked the snake with a stick. Dead. As a doornail. Willie stepped up, sniffed the carcass, and growled.

I stroked Rowdy's sweaty, shivering neck.

"He's not fond of snakes," I said, letting out a shaky laugh.

"No kidding," said Jasper.

I ran my hands up and down over Rowdy's front legs and picked up each hoof.

"Lucky he didn't get bit, but he's thrown a shoe," I

said, Rowdy's left front hoof held sole-up in my hand.

Jasper looked around until he found the horseshoe a couple yards off the trail. We had no hammer or horseshoe nails to put it back on.

"Rough country," Jasper said. "If he goes barefoot he'll be lame halfway down the mountain."

"Should have brought a boot," I shook my head. Riders often carried a rubber boot that slipped over the horse's hoof for just such emergencies. We hadn't thought of it.

I rummaged around in my saddlebag looking for anything that might work. Nothing.

Jasper took off his faded red sweatshirt. He bent over Rowdy's hoof, lifted it, and wrapped the sweatshirt around and underneath, like a cloth boot. "This'll protect him a little," he said. "Just need something to hold it on."

I unstrung a latigo strap off my saddle and laced it around Rowdy's ankle and up his leg, holding the sweatshirt in place.

"You saved me, Rowdy." I scratched my horse's chin and I whispered into his ear, "Thank God you're okay. Don't know what I'd do without you."

I kept turned sideways so Jasper couldn't see the tears running down my cheeks. I wiped my sleeve across my face and gave Rowdy another rub behind the ears.

When I led him a few feet down the trail, Rowdy high-stepped and stopped to nose the odd cloth "boot" on his foot. When he was walking normally again, I swung up into the saddle.

Jasper bent over the mangled snake. He pulled out his pocketknife and sawed through the snake's tough skin and spine and took the rattle. He handed it to me before getting back into the saddle himself.

"I wouldn't normally do that," he said. "It's disrespectful to an animal to show off that you killed it." We both knew people who killed every rattler they saw and kept their rattles as trophies.

"But you might want a reminder someday of how Rowdy saved you from getting snake-bit."

I examined the rattle before tucking it in my shirt pocket. "Eight buttons. That's eight years."

"But not going to get any older," Jasper said.

The cows had scattered in the noise and excitement of the snake stomping. Some were grazing on the hillsides and others stood in the dry creek bed. The calves hovered close to their mothers.

I looked back up the trail, scanning for any sign of the rustlers. A couple times I thought I saw a shadow or a movement, but it was just the trees waving their branches like arms as the wind picked up.

Would the rustlers be able to catch their horses? Would they come after us on foot if they had to? Just how mad were they?

It took a good half hour to gather the cattle and head them back down the trail.

"I've got a bad feeling," I said, looking over my shoulder again. "Like the rustlers are coming after us."

"Yep," Jasper said. "Why wouldn't they be?"

That didn't help. "Come on. Let's go. Let's go."

Finally, we were on our way again. I took another look behind us. No rustlers, but the sky was darkening around the edges, like a giant got hold of a black crayon and was scribbling out the sky.

"Storm coming," I said.

Jasper tipped back his hat and eyed the sky. "Yep."

I squeezed Rowdy into a trot. The last thing we needed was to get caught up here in a storm. We were all exhausted and wrung out. Getting drenched and frozen just might do us in worse than the rustlers.

As I urged a stray cow and her calf up out of a little side canyon, I wondered about that rattlesnake. It was way too cold up above for the creature to still be out. They were usually hibernating deep down in the ground by this time: old coyote dens, tunnels in boulder piles, cracks below cliffs, under old buildings.

I'd seen them in the late fall like this, though, soaking up the heat off the highway. It pays to be careful all year. You never know.

I'd heard a story from a guy on the road crew about finding a ball of hibernating snakes as big as a VW Bug when they blasted through rock for a road cut one winter. Snakes flew everywhere when the dynamite went off.

Nope. Didn't make sense for that snake to still be out. But, then again, if it had been warmer, the snake would have been livelier and faster and I'd probably be lying on a makeshift stretcher, all swollen up and hollering in pain while my friend hauled me down the mountain behind his horse.

I smiled over my shoulder at Jasper. Another disaster avoided.

He smiled back and started up singing again: "Ay, ay, ay, ay, canta y no llores, porque cantando se alegran, cielito lindo, los corazones."

Suddenly a clap of thunder drowned out his voice, the skies opened up, and an icy rain poured down on us.

Chapter 15

I guess that's what they mean when they say something put a damper on things, because the cold hard rain sure dampened my good mood. And the rest of me. And my horse.

I put my barn coat back on. It was wool and good for the cold but just soaked up the rain. Before we'd ridden another half mile, I felt as heavy as a wet sheep. I adjusted my hat brim to keep the rain off my neck, but it just ran down onto my back and soaked in.

In minutes, the bright autumn sky had turned dark gray over us. Jasper turned up his collar and pulled his hat low. "You can hardly see the mountain." He twisted in the saddle, nodding toward the cloudy sky behind us.

Sure enough, White Butte had disappeared in the sheets of rain pouring down. The pines around us started to groan and mutter as the wind snaked through their branches and bent their tops low.

Thunder rolled over the hills to the south. Willie stopped, lifted his head, and growled.

"He hates thunderstorms," Jasper said. "Probably thinks it's some big animal growling at us."

"Guess we should have brought slickers." Once again I felt like it was my fault we weren't prepared for the cold up on the plateau and now the wet. "Sorry."

The horses were soaked to the skin. Tigger's dun coat was dark brown; Rowdy's white patches shone bright and the brown ones nearly black.

The trail ran with ribbons of muddy water flowing down off the hill behind us. The horses slipped and slid in the red-brown mud. The mud up here is special: it was so slick that walking on it felt like ice-skating, but it also built up on your boots until you felt like you were walking on stilts.

I grabbed the saddle horn again and again as Rowdy caught himself up from falling. I added that to the list of dangers we faced; getting crushed under a horse that slipped in the mud.

To lighten things up as I clung to the saddle I said, "But I sure do like the smell of a good rain. The junipers and sage and pines make the air all sharp and clean."

Jasper tilted his hat brim back, shook his head, and smiled.

I shrugged and went on, "And we won't be meeting any more snakes in this weather."

Rowdy slid and stumbled down a rocky little chute. I grabbed the saddle horn again and leaned back, my legs stretched straight toward the front to shift my weight and help him keep his balance.

"Maybe we should shelter up and wait this out." Jasper was looking over his shoulder at Willie who trailed along at Tigger's heel like a giant black mop, soaked, head down, paws caked with red mud.

"I'd like to," I agreed, "but I doubt we could stop the cows from heading home now even if we tried. And the rain won't stop the men following us. If anything, they'll be madder from having to chase us through this storm."

I pictured us sheltered under the trees while our cows ran for home and a rustler pointed a gun at us and said, "Hands up!" Like in the movies.

"Nope. I think we better keep going."

Seemed like we were riding under a waterfall; the heaviest, darkest clouds hung right above us and showered our own personal deluge over our heads.

Thunder rumbled louder and closer. Out of the corner of my eye, I caught the glint of lightning snapping at the hilltops around us like a mad dog.

I whisper counted the seconds between the next flash and the clap of thunder that followed: one one thousand . . . two one thousand . . . three one thousand . . . BOOM!

Next flash: One one thousand . . . two one thousand . . . BOOM!

"Lightning's getting closer!" I hollered over the pounding rain and the wind.

The forest around us trembled as the wind blew harder, mixing pine needles and twigs with the rain that slammed us. Jasper had his red bandana pulled up over his face like a bandit. I did the same.

The rain dumping down on the mountains found its way into the creases between the hills. The dry creek beds that we'd passed on the way up now gurgled with dirty water, all flowing down to the river basin below.

Gullies ran across the trail where streams dodged out of their beds and took the straightest path down. Everything was going down, down, down the mountains.

Again and again, we urged the horses up and around rock slides and blown-down limbs that blocked the trail.

The sweatshirt-boot protecting Rowdy's shoeless hoof came loose and dragged, caked with mud. I rode him under a stand of aspen, took the cloth off, and shook off as much of the mud as I could, then retied it. I remounted and urged Rowdy down the trail until we were behind the herd again.

My face caught bits of mud and manure flying up from the cows' hooves as they hurried down the trail ahead of me. At least the bandana kept it out of my mouth, I thought. I didn't mind eating trail dust, but mud and cow crap was too much.

Jasper and Willie were heading strays up out of the gullies now, but most of the cattle were staying on the trail. In fact, they were close to stampeding down it, they were that spooked by the storm and that anxious to be safe and warm and fed back at the ranch.

So, we were all thundering down off the mountain when we hit the river, the Little Copper, the one that had been knee-deep when we'd waded across the day before. The cattle slid to a halt on the shore, bellowing and dodging back and forth on the bank.

The ford where we'd crossed was invisible; the river had grown huge and fast in the downpour and now overflowed its banks on both sides. The water roared deep and rough and brown.

I looked at Jasper in dismay. His mouth gaped open. His eyes were wide. He looked as terrified as I felt.

Chapter 16

This is where the ford was, right?" I asked. Jasper looked up and down the river, nodding at the trees, the rock cliff to our left. "Yep."

"So it'll be the shallowest, easiest place to cross, no matter how deep it's gotten."

"Yep. Rapids downstream, too many boulders upstream; not much choice."

I let out a snort of breath through my nostrils, trying to work up my determination. "Then we better just get to it."

Jasper smiled grimly. "Yep," he said once more.

I reined Rowdy to the right and gathered the cows and calves that had run the bank upstream, maybe looking for a better crossing or a bridge or something. Jasper rode downstream and gathered the rest and we aimed them at the ford and whooped and swung our ropes at their butts.

The first one brave enough to wade in was a big girl, ear-tag number 371. Good for you! I thought. I'm going to remember this one. Her calf bawled and went in after her.

When 371 and her calf reached the middle, the water lapped at the cow's sides and the calf was swimming. I could see the cow lose her footing in the deep water. She stretched her neck out to keep her nose above water and the calf did the same. The current carried them a few yards downstream before they stood and wallowed ashore.

The rest of the herd splashed in and waded and swam and bawled white-eyed until they trudged through the half drowned grass on the far side. All but one pair. The cow ran back and forth on the bank; her calf eyed the river and shook.

Mama cow finally got her front hooves in the water. Seemed like she was ready to brave the crossing but the calf was afraid.

I got down and hefted the calf up across my saddle. I untied Rowdy's sweatshirt-boot and hung it from the saddle horn, afraid it would come undone and trip him in the water. I swung up behind the squirming calf and held him tight against my body.

I didn't want to wait around getting more and more scared, and I didn't want to wait for the bad guys to catch up, so I squeezed Rowdy hard with my boots. He carried me and the calf into the river, the mother cow bellowing after us. Rowdy plowed carefully across, stumbling a little on the cobbled riverbed, forging a kitty-corner path upstream, to make up for the current.

When Rowdy reached deeper water, I hung on tight to the calf as the horse lurched and plunged through the waves. He found his footing in the shallower water and we came up safe on the other side. Mama cow pulled herself out of the water a few yards upstream.

I slid down onto solid ground and pulled the calf down and he ran to his mother. The cattle bellowed behind me in the grass, shaking their soaked hides like sodden dogs.

Rowdy stood beside me at the water's edge, blowing dirty river water from his nostrils and shivering. I tied his "boot" back on. The rain kept pounding down and we all stayed soaked no matter how much water we shook off.

Across the river, Jasper hoisted Willie up across his saddle as I'd done with the reluctant calf. He mounted up, one hand on the reins, the other stroking Willie's back. I could see his lips move as he spoke to the dog.

I shook the dirty water from my hair and wiped my face with my sleeve. It had been scary, but I'd done it. I felt a surge of pride. Jasper and I were pushing through all the obstacles to save the ranch. We really were heroes.

When I looked up again, I expected to see Jasper in the middle of the crossing, coming nearer. Instead, he still sat his horse on the far shore, Willie stretched over the saddle in front of him.

Jasper didn't meet my eyes, but kept looking up and down the shore, like he was deciding what to do. Like he had a choice.

"Don't think about it," I hollered over the roaring of the river, the pounding rain. "Just do it. Tig can swim. You'll be fine."

Minutes ticked by in my head. The cattle bunched up and looked downhill, toward home.

Jasper rode back and forth, reining his horse up and down the bank.

The cows started down the trail away from the river. We can't let them get too far ahead, I thought, or they'll scatter in the forest and we'll never find them before dark.

That's when I saw the figure walking out of the forest behind Jasper, soaked, like us, hunched and dripping in the cold rain.

It had to be one of the rustlers! He was on foot, so he

hadn't caught his horse. That was something. Probably caught up with us while we were battling the rattlesnake.

"Come on, Jasper!" I hollered. I pointed behind him.

He looked over his shoulder and startled in his saddle, jerking the reins as he saw the man coming out of the trees behind him.

"Jasper! Now!"

Jasper's eyes widened and his mouth fell open. He dug his heels into Tigger's sides. She hesitated, then lunged ahead, high-stepping into the frothy water. They went deeper and deeper, the water swirling around Tig's knees, then her belly.

I was more nervous for him than I'd been for myself and Rowdy. I whispered "Come on, come on," under my breath. The rustler raised his head and his eyes met mine across the roaring river. The hair on the back of my neck stood up.

The water just reached Jasper's stirrups when Tigger lost her footing and they went down.

I froze. "Drop your stirrups!" I yelled. If his feet got caught in the stirrups, he'd get tangled up and dragged under and drown.

Jasper and Willie disappeared under the horse. The current began to carry them all downstream, horse and rider and dog.

I quickly scanned the far bank, looking across the raging water for the stranger, but he was gone. Hiding in the brush? Gone to get the other two men? I put it out of my head. First things first: save Jasper and Willie and Tig.

I ran down the bank, trying to keep up as the horse and boy and dog thrashed and flailed their way down the river. I scrambled over fallen trees uprooted by the storm, clawed my way through washed up brush and rocks and debris, falling and getting up again and again, my eyes never leaving the river.

Tig's eyes rolled white and she screamed, that terrible, life-or-death cry a horse makes when it's completely terrified. Jasper and Willie disappeared between the horse's thrashing legs. They'd gone under.

I stopped to catch my breath and watched as the rough water broke open and Willy's big black body surfaced. The old dog strained to keep his head above the waves, but his nose kept disappearing under the churning white water. Then Jasper bobbed up a few feet behind him.

"Swim to shore!" I screamed. I ran and tripped and gasped.

But Jasper didn't head for shore. How could he? Willie was struggling. Jasper swam a few hard strokes and grabbed the dog's collar, then wrapped his arms around Willie's chest, holding his head above the waves.

The water roared louder. I looked downstream.

"Get out! The rapids!" I yelled.

Too late. Jasper clung to the big dog as they bumped and struggled, sucked down a narrow rock chute.

I lost sight of them as I fought through the flooded willows along the shore. Branches whipped my face as I slid and fell, then scrambled up and ran. When I emerged from the dense shrubs, my friend and his dog were nowhere in sight.

I heard a whinny and saw Tigger just below the rapids where the water spread and calmed. She was pulling herself up out of the water. She stood wide-legged and dazed, river water streaming from her neck and belly. A gash on her leg bled brilliant red.

That's when I saw Jasper's black hat floating down the river.

That's when I thought he was gone forever. I'd lost my best friend because I wanted to be a hero.

How could I have been so selfish? What would I say to his folks? How could I live with myself?

I paced up and down the bank, knee-deep in the cold muddy water, hollering his name and skimming my eyes over the rocks, the waves, the froth. I stopped to listen. Nothing but the roaring of the rapids, the drumbeat of rain, the rumble of thunder and crack of lightning.

Where had Jasper gone? I ran the possibilities through my head, hating them all. He'd hit his head on a rock and drowned. He had gotten caught in the branches of a downed tree and drowned. Saving Willie had exhausted him and he drowned. . . .

"Hey!" Jasper's voice skittered weakly over the water, as if from far away. "Cassie! Help!"

My heart leaped into my throat. "Jasper! Where are you?" I yelled my loudest, cupping my hands around my mouth. No answer.

The river followed a bend just downstream from me and I couldn't see beyond the shrubs lining the bank. I stumbled through the underbrush, stopping to listen for his voice. I was soaked to the skin and shivering, but I didn't feel the cold. Jasper was alive! I just had to find him.

As I rounded a gravel point I spotted the blue of his torn coat among the gray and white and brown of river and rock.

He was hunkered on a flat boulder in the middle of the swollen river, his arms wrapped tight around his dog. The river split around him, roaring deep and fast on either side. His face was as white as the foaming water.

Chapter 17

Jasper!" Relief washed over me, just seeing him alive. "Are you hurt?"

He looked up and waved with one arm, the other still clinging tight to Willie. I couldn't tell if he was crying or if it was just the rain and river water running down his face. My own tears ran hot over my cheeks. I didn't care if he saw me cry.

"I'm okay," his voice trembled, so I doubted he was telling me the truth.

"Hang on," I yelled. "I'll figure something out."

I looked around: nothing but rocks, willows, raging water. How could I get him to shore? He looked too exhausted to swim, most likely in shock. And he might be hurt, even though he said he was okay; broken bones from the rapids, maybe a concussion.

The water was deep here and still fast, though not as rocky as the worst of the rapids upstream. He might make it if he just swam across. Still, he'd have to hang on to Willie; I didn't want to chance it.

"I'm going to get a rope." I headed back upstream, eyeing the far bank. No sign of the man across the river. Could be behind the willows. Could have given up. Unlikely.

I found Tigger stumbling through the coyote willows, her head hanging in exhaustion, her eyes glazed over. I stroked her neck. I wanted to comfort her, to check her wounded leg, but there was no time. I had to help Jasper.

I tied her to a tree and went back to the ford to get Rowdy. The cows were gone. That was the least of my problems. We'd have to catch up with them later.

One more time, I was thankful that my horse was good and loyal: he hadn't followed the cattle toward home; he was waiting for me where I'd left him. I picked up his reins and led him through the willows to Tigger.

I led both horses downstream to the shore across from Jasper. He hadn't moved at all. Willie was slumped in his arms.

I unlaced the latigo that held Jasper's rope near the saddle horn and undid my rope, as well.

I stood on the shore and measured the distance between Jasper and me with my eyes. There was about thirty feet of deep, fast water between us. Jasper was the better roper of the two of us, so I almost wished it was me on the rock and him throwing the rope. Almost.

I tied the two ropes together with a half hitch and pulled the knot tight. I walked upstream a few yards so if I missed the current would catch the rope and carry it by him. At least that was my plan.

I coiled the ropes into loose loops and twirled about five feet of one end over my head. "Here it comes!" I yelled and flung the end of the rope as far out over the water as I could. It fell short of Jasper's rock and splashed into the water. The current carried it downstream and back to shore.

I hauled it in hand over hand and tried again, flinging the wet rope with all my strength. Same thing.

"Tie something on it," Jasper yelled. "A piece of wood or a rock for weight."

I hunted around in the grass until I found a foot-long chunk of juniper. I tied it to the end of the rope. Then I whirled the piece of wood around and around over my head and let go.

The wood landed just upstream from Jasper's rock and the current carried it down past him. He let go of

Willie, lay down on the boulder, and reached out to grab for it. It floated about two inches out of his reach and on downstream. I pulled it back to the bank.

Why couldn't I throw like Jasper!?

As I wound up to throw it again, a movement on the far bank caught my eye. A flash of red and blue. A dirty plaid shirt, a hat slouched low in the rain, a dark beard split by a nasty grin.

I couldn't hear him over the waves, but he seemed to say, "Gotcha!" as he raised a rifle, pointing it toward the river, toward Jasper hunched on the rock. He squinted along the barrel.

I threw with all my strength. The chunk of wood with the rope trailing it flew across the water. This time Jasper lunged for it. His feet slipped and he fell to his knees, inches from the rock's edge.

"Got it!" He held the chunk of wood up, triumphant.

BANG!

A gunshot blasted and a bullet skittered off the rocks a few feet from Jasper. The guy was shooting at him! More shots echoed across the water.

BANG! BANG!

"Get down!" I hollered. He dropped down onto the rock, sheltering Willie with his body. Jasper's face went white.

I looked around but there were no trees big enough to tie my end of the rope to, just the scrubby bushes. I had to find something quick!

"Come here, Rowdy." He lifted his head and stepped up to me. My hands shook as I tied the rope to his saddle horn and tightened his girth up snug.

The guy on the far shore was looking down, fiddling with his gun. Reloading? Or maybe it was jammed. With any luck. . . .

I watched Jasper wrap his end of the rope around his chest and up under his arms and knot it. He held Willie tight around the dog's middle with one arm. Jasper had to have been scared. I'd have been petrified out there. But he seemed to have gained some courage by having to save Willie, too.

"Ready?" he shouted over the roar of the water.

"Ready," I shouted back.

I held Rowdy's reins under his chin and backed him up until the rope went taut.

Jasper looked over his shoulder at the man still fumbling with the gun on the bank. He eased into the water, holding the rope with one hand and Willie with the other.

The current grabbed them right away and began to sweep them in a big arc downstream and toward shore. They disappeared under the water and bobbed back up, sputtering and coughing. Jasper's legs churned under him, as he tried to stay at the surface.

I backed Rowdy up a few more steps and they swung closer. The knot between the two ropes strained. Had I used the best knot? Would it hold or would it come loose and send Jasper and Willie rushing downstream?

Jasper grimaced as the loop around his chest tightened. Willie twisted in his arms. The poor blind dog must have been terrified.

The man on the far bank shouted something and waved the rifle in the air.

"Can you stand?" I yelled to my friend.

Jasper seemed to be feeling around with his feet while the rope swung him closer to shore. "Not yet!"

A few more feet. A few more seconds. When I looked up at the far bank again, the man with the rifle was gone. Was he going back for the others? Was he trying to cross the river? Either way, we didn't have much time.

I held Rowdy's reins and backed him a few more steps.

Jasper thrashed around until suddenly his feet touched bottom. He stood, unsteady in the current. He held on to the rope, but pushed Willie ahead of him. The old dog struggled and splashed until he stumbled up onto the gravel shore and collapsed.

Jasper trudged the last few feet, fell to his knees, and crawled out of the water. He crumpled in the sand next to his dog.

Jasper lay there a long minute, panting, and then sat up. He felt Willie's legs and sides. He hugged his neck and stroked him.

The rain poured over us. The river roared and spit, like it was mad that they'd escaped.

"Any broken bones?" I scanned the far bank again looking for the shooter. No sign. That was almost worse; I wanted to know where he was.

"Don't know. Too tired," answered Jasper, his eyes closed, his fingers kneading Willie's soaked fur. "Do you see him, the rustler?"

"No." I shook my head. My insides were roiling like the river. "But I know he's out there. And maybe the others."

"They can't cross without the horses; no way," Jasper said.

"Come on." I nudged his boot with mine. Jasper groaned.

I grabbed his hand and dragged him to his feet. "We can't stay here. The other rustlers may be right behind this guy, and they might have the horses."

Jasper stood shakily.

"There's something else," I added, though I hated to pile bad news on him. "Tigger's hurt her leg."

I showed him the flap of skin, the open wound. "She's limping, but it's not broken."

Jasper examined his horse's leg, felt the bone up and down, tried to lift the hoof but she wouldn't pick it up for him.

"We'll doctor it later," I said. "Right now, we have to put some distance between us and the guy with the gun."

The wet brush slapped our faces as we hurried through the brush, leading the horses upstream. Jasper kept talking behind me. "Cass, when Tig slipped and I was under her, underwater, I thought I was a goner."

"I thought you were too."

"Then when I was bouncing off the rocks down the rapids, I thought I was done for."

"Me too." We crashed along the brushy bank upstream.

Jasper went on: "Then, I was on the rock and my whole body hurt and the water was so fast; I couldn't figure how I was going to make it to shore. And then the guy with the gun. . . . If I'd stayed out there, he would have got me for sure. You saved me."

I shook my head, pushing aside a branch. "I didn't really save you, Jasper. It was me who almost got you killed in the first place." I couldn't look at him. . . . "I was the one who brought you up here after my cows. I wanted to be a hero. I was totally selfish."

Now it was Jasper shaking his head at me. "Cass, you were trying to take responsibility for your family. If it was my ranch and my herd, I would have done the same," he said. "And you would have come along and helped."

"That's true," I agreed.

"And then I would have been the one throwing the rope to you . . ." Jasper gave me a wrung-out smile, ". . . and it would have landed on the first try."

"Very funny." Jasper winced as I punched him in the shoulder.

Chapter 18

When we were away from the river and hidden by the pines, I felt safe enough to stop and take care of Tig's leg.

"Hold her," I said. "I'll get it cleaned up. And keep an eye out for the rustlers."

I didn't like the delay, but it was the only thing to do. I dug in my saddlebag and pulled out the little white metal box that held our first aid kit. At least I'd remembered to pack a few important things, if not raincoats and warm clothes.

Jasper held Tigger's reins, scanning the far shore, shifting from one foot to the other.

I poured springwater over the wound. Tigger jerked back, trying to escape the sting. "Hold her tight," I said picking out some gravel with my fingernails. It looked bad. Could she even make it down the mountain? We couldn't leave her. Never.

"Easy girl," Jasper stroked her neck and held the reins tight under her chin.

I squeezed antibiotic ointment on the red, raw skin, and pushed the flap of hide gently back over it. Then I wrapped the leg in gauze and taped it with white first aid tape.

"I have an idea." I used the rest of the roll of tape to secure the sweatshirt protecting Rowdy's shoeless hoof, wrapping it around and around his leg.

"I feel bad," I said. "Both horses will be limping off this mountain. And you don't look so hot, either." I hung my head, feeling guilty that I'd put us all in so much danger. "You almost got shot and drowned."

"You wanted to save the ranch," Jasper said. "Remember why we're doing all this. We have to stay focused on the herd." He looked over his shoulder, across the river. "Forget the rustlers. They won't make it across. Maybe they'll give up. Or try to swim it and drown."

I nodded. If we could just get the cattle home and not lose any of us on the way, it might all be worth it.

"You ride Rowdy," I said. "I'll walk Tigger, to rest her leg."

Jasper shook his head. "No, I can walk my own

horse." He took the reins from me.

"Suit yourself. Thought you might be too tired from your swim."

"Ha-ha. You're sooo funny." Jasper staggered down the trail leading his limping horse. Willie followed, head low, at Tigger's heel.

Jasper started to sing, but seemed too tired even to do that and switched to humming instead.

We made our way through the trees and the rain let up. I tried to breathe the sharp pine scent, the rain-soaked juniper, to calm myself. Jasper kept walking Tig though I offered to trade places with him a couple times.

I kept looking ahead for the cows and back for the rustlers. Nobody was behind us that I could see.

The trailside was trampled and we kicked our way through a lot of cow pies. The herd was up ahead somewhere. Not too far, I hoped.

"Tigger's having a hard time." Jasper had stopped behind me. His forehead furrowed up as he squatted and ran a hand over Tig's wounded leg. "She's hardly putting any weight on it."

I swung down and squatted next to him. Her leg steamed hot under my hand. "Infection." I shook my head. "We have to get her to a vet. Just keep going slow."

I mounted back up. Could this get any worse? What

if Tigger was lame for life? The slower we went, the easier for the rustlers to catch us. This was all my fault.

Seemed like we'd gone miles before I finally heard a calf bawling for its mother and the mama cow answering back.

"Hear that, Jas?"

"Uh huh!" He grinned and gave a tug on Tigger's reins to speed her up. She limped a little faster. She was a good, brave girl. I squeezed Rowdy into a trot.

We came around a rock outcropping to find the herd fanned out across a meadow, grazing. They looked up from chewing the bunchgrass when they saw us.

The sun broke through the clouds, slanting through the treetops on the hills to the west. It was getting late.

"What do you think? Four, maybe five o'clock?"

"Sunset's early this time of year," Jasper replied, shading his eyes with his free hand, the other still holding Tig's reins. "I make it closer to three, three-thirty."

"Our folks will start looking for us if we're not back by dark."

"If we'd really been camping, we'd be getting home about now."

We needed to keep going, but Jasper looked dead on his feet, and both horses walked with their heads low, tripping and stumbling. They'd been through a lot.

"Rest a minute while the cows are eating?" I asked, though I knew the answer. I wanted to put the rustlers out of my mind for a few minutes. I told myself they were stuck on the far side of the river. I wanted it to be true.

Jasper hooked Tig's reins over his saddle horn and dropped into the grass with a sigh. "Don't have to ask me twice," he said. Willie plunked down next to Jasper and stretched out in the stubbly grass, resting his head on his paws.

I swung down. "Sleeping on the cold ground, riding so far in this rough country: I feel like I got run over by a truck! Every bone in my body hurts." I dug out the last of the pemmican and a bottle of water I'd filled at the spring on the plateau that morning.

"It seems like weeks ago we were up there stealing our cattle back." I nodded toward the mountains behind us, passing him the pemmican.

"I feel a hundred years older."

I settled into the grass beside him. "Pa'll be proud, when he gets over being mad." I chewed slowly and swallowed a slug of water and watched the horses browse. I couldn't help glancing up the trail behind us. Still nothing. No one.

"And you can stay on the ranch and won't have to move to the city and run around in high heels and nail polish." Jasper followed my gaze and scanned the timber at our backs.

I laughed. "Oh yeah, I can just see me doing that. No, even if I had to move to the city, I'd still be me, still go to class in jeans and boots. I wouldn't care if everyone made fun of me."

I thought about what was important to me, my horse and the ranch and Pa and Jasper and even Fran and added: "At least I know who I am."

Jasper nodded, looking thoughtful, maybe thinking about who he was and what mattered most to him.

I went on: "I'll be the cowgirl who rode into the mountains with her friend and fought off wild horses and a crazy miner and a rattlesnake to steal our cattle back from rustlers and at least try to save the ranch."

Jasper nodded again. "Don't forget about saving me and Willie off that rock in the middle of the river."

I shook my head. "You would have been able to swim to shore once you'd rested up."

"Whatever," he said. "Your little speech is inspiring, but we may have some guys with guns after us. I think we better go."

The rain had slackened into a slow, cold drizzle while we'd been sitting.

"Yep." I climbed into the saddle. Seemed like a long

ways up. My bones ached and my muscles felt like jelly. I let out a little moan as I hauled my body up, but covered it with a cough.

Jasper stood and checked Tig's leg again. "It's swollen." He gently poked at the puffy skin above and below the bandage.

"I'm sorry, Jasper." I really, really was. "She has to keep going."

The shadows were deeper between the trees. I thought of being out here in the dark, hunted by the rustlers.

"How mad do you think our folks will be?" Jasper pulled gently on Tigger's reins. The mare took a tentative step forward, then another. She settled into a slow, stumbling walk.

"Mad as they were when we stole Glory?" Jasper asked.

"Probably. Probably more, if we tell them everything. I'm thinking it might be smart to leave some things out."

"Like, maybe say, 'We rode up, found the cows, and brought them home.'"

"Yeah, something like that."

The brush cracked behind us, just off the trail. We both jerked around to face the sound. Willie hackled up and growled low.

Chapter 19

I squinted hard into the darkness under the trees. Willie growled louder and lunged forward.

"Grab him!" I shouted, but it was too late. Willie charged into the underbrush at the edge of the meadow. He moved so fast, you wouldn't know he was old, and blind.

Jasper dropped Tigger's reins and ran after his dog. "Willie! No!"

A horrible snarl broke the afternoon air. Then some barking and a loud yelp. Jasper shouted for Willie. The brush shook and snapped.

I scrambled down from the saddle and took off after them.

Just as I reached the brush, a furry snarling ball rolled out at me. Willie and a gray-brown coyote had each other by the throats.

Jasper grabbed at Willie's collar.

"No, Jasper! You'll get bit!" I snatched at his coat sleeve and hung on.

The coyote jumped when I shouted. He let go of Willie and wriggled free from the dog's grasp faster than I could blink. It was one thing to fight a dog, but another to face two humans. He tucked his tail between his legs and ran.

Jasper dropped to his knees and hugged Willie. "First he almost drowns in the river and now this!" Tears rolled down Jasper's cheeks. "I'm so sorry, Willie."

Willie's right ear was torn. He shook his head and bright blood sprayed across Jasper's face. Jasper hugged the dog tighter.

Willie strained after the coyote. If Jasper hadn't held him, I was sure he would have chased the animal off into the forest.

"It's all right, Jas." I knelt next to him and held Willie still so I could check him all over. "It's just his ear. They bleed a lot. He's okay."

My assurance wasn't working: Jasper couldn't seem to stop crying. It was all catching up with him, I suppose. The long hard ride, the rustlers, the river, exhaustion, fear, and now this.

I put an arm around his shoulder. "It's okay. Willie's

okay. Tig's gonna be all right, too. I promise. We're almost home, Jasper. Just a little farther. But I need you. I can't get the cows down by myself." I pulled him to his feet.

Jasper wiped his streaming nose on his coat sleeve. Willie stood with his head up and his feet braced wide, like he'd just won a championship fight.

"Look," I pointed at Willie. "He's proud of himself. He feels fine."

"I guess."

I looked around for the rustlers again. "C'mon, buddy. Let's bring 'em home."

We clucked and whistled and got the cattle all going down the trail again. They were anxious to get going and jogged along at a good pace.

When we got near the mining town, I wished we could just hop over it and not chance seeing Crazy Ellie again.

The cattle barreled through, there being no grass in the barren clearing to entice them. Jasper and I hurried as well, heads down. I urged Rowdy into a weary lope and Jasper tugged at Tigger's reins, leading the mare as fast as she could hobble.

"Hold on there!" Ellie appeared from behind the dilapidated store. She moved faster than I thought possible for an old lady. All at once, she was in front of us, blocking our path. Ellie grabbed Tigger's reins and held tight.

Willie growled softly from his spot at Tigger's heel. The cows kept going through the ghost town and down the road toward home. Without us. Again.

We were getting so close and now we were stalled out again. I looked up the trail behind us for the man with the evil grin and the rifle, maybe even his two partners in crime. I could almost feel them catching up. We had to get out of here. Now!

"I see you got your cows back," Ellie croaked.

Jasper perked up. "Yeah, we did. Some cattle thieves had them! And Willie and I almost drowned in the river, and one of the rustlers followed us and shot at me! Cassie saved us."

He sounded like he was catching up an old friend on all the news.

"Come on, Jasper. We gotta go." I rode up next to him and pulled the reins. "Let go, Ellie."

"Let go? You got more important people to see than old Ellie?" she said.

"We've got to get the cattle home before dark. And I don't want to give those rustlers a chance to catch up. We gotta go. Now!"

"I ain't afraid of no rustlers," Ellie growled at me, lifting her rifle with her free hand. "I can hold 'em off for you. Plus your horse is lame." This she said to Jasper.

"Yeah, but she'll make it. It's not much farther," I said. "We're going." I pulled the reins out of her hand and began leading Jasper and Tig away from the camp.

"Hold your horses, missy," she hollered at my back. "I got a salve that will fix her right up. She'll be good as new."

Jasper looked at me, his eyes pleading. "It'll only take a minute, Cass," Jasper said. "And she's limping so bad."

I looked up the trail again. Maybe the rustlers couldn't make it across the river after all. I looked down the trail. The cows were gone. I ached to go after them.

Ellie hobbled to her cabin and came back with a little jar of yellow scum and a long strip of white cloth "This'll do the trick. Numbs the pain. Heals infection. Good as new."

Jasper stroked Tig's neck as Ellie unwound the dirty bandage, tenderly dabbed the ointment into the wound, and folded the skin back over it. Then she gently wrapped it again with a clean bandage. I had to give it to her; she seemed to know what she was doing.

She screwed the lid on the jar and handed it to Jasper. "Put some on every day 'til it's scabbed over."

"Thanks, Ellie." Jasper carefully tucked the jar into his saddlebag.

"You," she turned to me, "need to let up."

"What?"

"Take some help when it comes your way. Don't need to do everything alone. You'll get home all right."

Jasper led Tigger down the trail after me and Rowdy.

"I'll come back and help dig out that gold," Jasper hollered over his shoulder. He and Ellie waved at each other.

"What did she mean by that?" I asked.

"Just what she said, I guess. Don't look a gift horse in the mouth?" He was grinning.

"Are you really going to come back and help her?"

"Of course. And we'll find gold and I'll be rich. And if you're nice, I'll share some of my fortune with you."

I was still thinking about Ellie's advice when I heard her shouting behind us.

I looked over my shoulder. Ellie was pointing her rifle at the man in the slouched hat. He was backed up against the shack with his hands in the air. His own rifle lay on the ground between him and Ellie.

"Go! Go! Go!" I yelled.

I wanted to kick Rowdy into a trot, but Jasper and Tigger and Willie were limping along behind, so I held us to a fast walk. I had to trust that Ellie would keep him there long enough for us to escape.

We followed the double track through the old gate and around the bend and down the mountain. When we'd put half a mile or so between us and the mining town, I finally exhaled the breath I'd been holding.

"See?" Jasper said. "She isn't so crazy after all." And I did see. Jasper was right. Ellie had saved us.

Chapter 20

We came down off the mine road and onto the gravel. The cows trotted along like they could smell hay and shelter and home. The sky to the west colored pink and orange. Sunset. The sky darkened to the east.

As glad as I'd been to leave the road the last time we were here, to escape the notice of anyone driving by, I was that glad to see "civilization" now. The rustlers wouldn't dare attack us here, where they could be seen by witnesses. They'd have to turn back.

I straightened up in the saddle. We'd done it. Jasper must have been feeling the same triumph, because he started singing louder than ever:

"De la Sierra Morena, cielito lindo, vienen bajando, Un par de ojitos negros, cielito lindo, de contrabando. . . ."

"What's that song mean, anyway?"

"It's an old song from Mexico. 'Down from the Sierra Moreno Mountains, pretty little darling, they come, a pair of little black eyes, pretty little darling, that are being smuggled. . . .'"

"Teach me the words."

We went along singing and laughing at my awful Spanish and lousy singing.

"¡Qué terrible!" Jasper shook his head and laughed. I reached down and smacked him with my hat.

We were nearly home. We'd saved the cattle and the ranch. Everything was going to be all right. I stood up in my stirrups and whooped.

"YEEHAW!!!"

Even though he was still on foot, leading his limping horse, Jasper waved his hat over his head and yipped like a coyote.

Dusk had a good hold on the valley when we hit the highway. Not a good time to move cattle down the road; too hard to see.

"Sunday night," Jasper was reading my mind again. "Shouldn't be much traffic."

"Nope."

I yipped and hollered and swung my rope, and the worn-out cows and their exhausted calves trotted the few miles down the highway. We got lucky—no cars came along. It seemed like hours, but was probably just minutes, when we finally turned them off onto our road.

Nighthawks swooped up mosquitoes back and forth over the creek and mourning doves cooed on the wires. A coyote wailed from a hilltop to the east. Another answered from the next ridge over. The mountains we'd traveled and struggled through faded pale and distant behind us.

"Home stretch," Jasper smiled. "Good thing; I think my boots are worn through from walking and I can hardly see the cows."

Darkness nearly swallowed them: they were a ghost herd groaning and tramping ahead of us.

I nodded, suddenly so weary I could have fallen out of my saddle. They say that excitement keeps you going, adrenalin rushing through your veins, then, when you make it wherever you're going, you crash. That was me.

We followed the cattle down Burnt Ranch Road, the home stretch, like Jasper had said.

I felt like everything went into slow motion, then, like we'd been plodding down this road behind the ghost herd forever. I watched Jasper stumble and figured he was wrung-out, too.

"Let me lead her," I said again. "You ride for a while."

Jasper shook his head. "I'm okay. She's my horse. I'll lead her home."

On and on we went, though it was only a few miles. On and on and then we rounded the bend in the road where the hills held our ranch like a cupped hand. The kitchen light blushed a friendly yellow through the curtains. Fran was probably washing up the dishes.

Pa stood on the porch with a "What the . . . ?" look on his face as the cattle streamed past him and into the barnyard. They knew exactly where they were going, remembering the cold water waiting in the troughs, the piles of hay forked down from the loft. The bummer calves in the next corral bawled at the mama cows and their calves.

I sat up tall in the saddle. We'd done what we set out to do. Pride swelled in my chest. My head felt light, my lungs full, my body tingling. Jasper was wide awake now and grinning up at me.

I waved at Pa and he halfway lifted his hand like he couldn't believe what he was seeing. Fran came out and stood beside him on the porch, wiping her soapy hands on her jeans.

I hopped down and opened the corral and Jasper drove the cows in, although they didn't take much convincing.

When I'd shut the gate behind the last rump, I led

Rowdy to the water trough in the barnyard and he sucked down a long drink.

I left him tied there, dozing on his feet and took the long walk across to the porch, not knowing if I was in the worst trouble yet, worse than the rustlers or rattlesnake or the river, or if I was the hero I felt like.

Pa still stood with his mouth hanging open.

Fran's eyes were huge in the porch light. "Cassie, what did you do?" she asked.

"Jasper and I brought the herd down from the mountains," I said.

"By yourselves?!" Pa was shaking his head. "Cassie, you shouldn't. . . . I can't believe. . . . you said you were camping. . . ."

Jasper came up onto the porch and stood beside me. He looked awful in the porch light: his hair tangled and matted, his face and arms cut and bruised.

"Maybe we shouldn't have, sir, but we did," Jasper said. It wasn't like him to speak up like that to my pa, to anyone's pa. Or maybe it was like him, now.

"I did it to save the ranch, Pa."

He just kept shaking his head.

"Well, you may have done that," Pa said. "Still, it wasn't for you to do. It was a dangerous stunt, you two going up there alone."

"Maybe." I said. I wasn't about to tell him all the things that had gone wrong. But even with all that, I knew we'd chosen rightly. Maybe I'd be in the worst trouble ever, grounded for life. But I couldn't see how I could have not done it. I looked at the ground and waited.

Pa sighed. "Put your horse away. Let's give Jasper and Willie a ride home in the truck. Tigger can stay with Rowdy tonight." He put his arm across my shoulder. I felt a rush of relief as his face slackened, like the anger was draining away.

"No thank you, sir." Jasper shook his head. "I'll make it on my own."

He turned to lead Tigger home. "Ven, Willie."

"Thank you so much, Jasper. You're the best friend ever," I said.

He smiled. "I know," he said.

I stood and listened to Tigger's hooves crunching down the gravel drive. Jasper started up singing his Spanish song.

"Canta y no llores, porque cantando se alegran. . . ."

I walked Rowdy to the barn and put him in a stall to rest. "We did it, Rowdy," I said. I rubbed his long nose and gave him an extra helping of oats and went in to tell Pa and Fran most of the story.

Epilogue

How did it all end up? We got to keep the ranch, which made all the trouble and danger worthwhile. Pa was more astounded than angry. I'd catch him looking at me like he didn't recognize me, like I'd changed that much. Maybe I looked like I'd grown up all at once. I felt like it.

Fran was disappointed that she wouldn't be meeting all those city boys, since we didn't have to move. But I think even she's a little proud of me too.

Jasper's parents swung back and forth between being hopping mad and sobbing grateful that he was okay. Rowdy got new shoes, and Tig's leg healed up.

The rustlers never got caught, except for the one unlucky enough to end up on the wrong end of Ellie's rifle. She won't tell us what happened to him. I like to think she's got him working in the mine now. I guess the other two are still out there, looking for a chance to steal someone else's cows.

Jasper and I did go back to the gold mine: him to find gold, me to keep an eye on him. So far, his share of the gold he and Ellie found is a few more flakes sparkling in a little glass bottle. Jasper says that when it comes to gold, where there's a little there's a lot, so I think he still intends to strike it rich.

Pa said the bummer calves we'd vaccinated were mine and Jasper's for real now. He said we could pick another calf to add to the group every year; our own herd is up and growing!

Brave mama cow, number 371, the first to cross the river, got to stay at the ranch and became our family milk cow.

Me, I like to ride up to the ridge between our ranch and Jasper's. I look down at the river winding through the valley, the cattle we saved grazing in the pasture, the fences and barns and our house. I feel pride rising up in my chest knowing I had a hand in keeping us here on the land.

Spanish Glossary

Spanish	English
Claro	Yes; of course
Estoy intentando	I'm trying
Ven	Come (here)
¿Estás bien?	Are you okay?
¡No es posible!	That can't be!
Entonces	So; then
Pobrecito	Poor thing/guy
¿Qué pasó?	What happened?
¡Vamanos!	Let´s go!
No lo hagas	Don't do it

¡Es suficiente! .... That's enough!

Para servirle .... At your service

¡No entres a lo
que huele mal! .... Don't go into the stink!

Ven acá ....Come here

Estamos aquí .... We're (over) here

¡Hace mucho frío! ....It's very cold!

Tapaderas .... Leather hood that
covers the stirrups

Lo siento ....I'm sorry

¿Qué es eso? ....What is that?

Tu estás encargado del .... You're in charge
lugar y necesitas   and you need to take
cuidar muy bien   good care of the place.

Cassie & Jasper: Kidnapped Cattle
Study Guide Questions

1. Cassie and Jasper lie to their families to get away for the weekend and rescue the cattle. Is it ever okay to lie and deceive? Even for a very good reason?

2. By taking on Cassie's cause to save her family's ranch, Jasper faces life-or-death situations: Would you risk everything to help a friend, as Jasper does?

3. Which do you rely on more, your friends or your family? What do you get from one that you don't get from the other?

4. Do you think Cassie went after the cattle to be a hero or to help her family? Was she being selfish? Why did Jasper go along? Would you have gone?

5. Cassie wants to stay on the ranch forever. Fran would love to move to the city and experience new things. Who are you more like?

6. The kids could have given up or gone for help when they encountered the rustlers. Was their choice the best? What would you have done in their place?

7. Jasper considers Willie a member of his family. The horses, Rowdy and Tigger, make the cattle rescue possible. How important are animals in your life? Do you think of them as pets or as family members? Why?

8. Do you know anyone like the miner, Ellie, who lives apart or differently from everyone else? How do you feel about her and her choices?

9. What personal qualities (courage, recklessness, humor) helped the kids overcome the obstacles they faced?

10. Cassie and Jasper approach problems differently. How do you deal with difficulties, by charging ahead like Cassie or by thinking them through and acting carefully like Jasper?

11. The kids agree to tell their parents only part of the story, not revealing all the trouble and danger they experienced. Why? Was that the right thing to do?

12. How might the kids' lives have changed if they'd

been unsuccessful and come back without the cattle? Would they have regretted trying? Have you tried and failed at something important? Are you glad you tried?

13. If one of the kids had been seriously hurt, would the journey have been worth it? Have you ever done something dangerous or against the rules for a good cause?